Battleground:
Nova Scotia

Battleground:
Nova Scotia

The British, French, and First Nations at
War in the Northeast 1675–1760

RONALD E. GAFFNEY

BATTLEGROUND: NOVA SCOTIA: THE BRITISH, FRENCH, AND FIRST NATIONS AT WAR IN THE NORTHEAST 1675–1760

This book is written to provide information and motivation to readers. Its purpose is not to render any type of psychological, legal, or professional advice of any kind. The content is the sole opinion and expression of the author, and not necessarily that of the publisher.

Copyright © 2019 by Ronald E. Gaffney

Printed in the United States of America.

ISBN   978-1-64552-085-6   (Paperback)
ISBN   978-1-64552-086-3   (Digital)

Lettra Press books may be ordered through booksellers or by contacting:

Lettra Press LLC
18229 E 52nd Ave.
Denver City, CO 80249
1 303 586 1431 | info@lettrapress.com
www.lettrapress.com

Contents

Preface

For a number of years now, I have contemplated writing a book about what I believe to be the most interesting era in the history of the Maritime region—the colonial wars that raged from the late 1600s until 1760. I have now accomplished that task with the help and support of a number of people, most especially my wonderful wife, Cindy, my sons, Thomas and Charles, and their children (mainly with technical support, given their computer genius). I also wish to thank my sister, Susan Jones, who kindly reviewed the finished product and made many helpful suggestions toward the editing and content.

My purpose in writing this book is to broaden the general public's understanding of a fascinating time in our regional "saga" and introduce that public to the riveting events, colorful people, and fascinating places that contributed to our Maritime story. I am certain that many readers will be surprised by some of the details of our early history that are rarely the object of examination. At times, this is a very dark story, but it is also a tale of courage, endurance, and bold action. I hope that those who take an interest in this story will further examine the colonial histories of the Maritime region and the state of Maine.

Introduction

I live in Maritime Canada. In this relatively peaceful corner of the world, Maritimers rarely consider the fact that "old" Nova Scotia was once a battleground. When I say "old" Nova Scotia, I mean, roughly speaking, what are today the Canadian provinces of New Brunswick and Nova Scotia, absent Cape Breton, and a portion of the state of Maine in the United States of America. The events that took place on this "battleground" still reverberate today. The evolution of British, Acadian, and First Nation societies in Eastern Canada began in the crucible of more than a half century of warfare. Those societies live with the consequences of that conflict to this very day. It is impossible to understand the English, French, and First Nations cultures in the Maritimes and their perspectives on current events without first understanding this violent past.

European exploration and settlement, religious and economic rivalries, and the quest by aboriginal peoples to maintain some semblance of independence combined to fan the flames of war.

The seventeenth and eighteenth centuries were punctuated by episodes of ethnic violence in the Maritimes. This violence played no small part in the 1755 Expulsion and grand "diaspora" of the French-speaking Acadian population residing in the region. Acadians now living around the world (including the famous "Cajuns" of Louisiana) are keenly aware that their culture and way of life were once violently ripped from the bosom of their adopted homeland. The Acadian people, who came to the Maritime region in the early 1600s, lived side by side in relative peace with the aboriginal tribes who had made that place their home for ten thousand years. But that peace was soon shattered by English raids and later by a slow-moving British invasion. By the 1750s, a full-blown battle for supremacy was underway for control of "old" Nova Scotia.

Today, we call the aboriginal tribes of the Maritimes "First Nations". They were and are the three tribes whose members hunted, fished, and travelled with one another for centuries before Europeans arrived:

1. The Mi'kmaq of mainland Nova Scotia, Cape Breton, the east coast of New Brunswick, and the Gaspé region of Québec;
2. The Maliseet or "Wolastoqiyik" of the St. John River Valley;
3. The Maliseet's less numerous ethnic relatives, the Passamaquoddy of "down east" Maine and southwestern New Brunswick.

These tribes were not only familiar with the vast expanse of their own exclusive territories but travelled to the southwest and forged trade and military alliances with other Algonquian-speaking tribes living along the northeastern coast of America. Both the Mi'kmaq and Passamaquoddy were coastal peoples whose bark wigwams and lodges dotted the coves and lands close to river estuaries in the region. The Maliseet were mainly a river people who liked to build their villages near the confluence of two river systems, close to "portage" routes, which then allowed those rivers to be used as "water highways." The Mi'kmaq and Maliseet were both known to have constructed log palisades at some village sites to protect themselves from their enemies.

The Maliseet
[Provincial Archives of New Brunswick, George Taylor Fonds P5 – 170]

The Mi'kmaq, Maliseet, and Passamaquoddy were warrior nations. While in pre-Contact times (before 1605) it seems that they rarely warred among themselves, they did have a history of fighting other neighboring First Nations especially the dreaded Mohawk, an Iroquoian people. When Europeans arrived in significant numbers in the early 1600s, the tribes quickly acquired firearms through trade and soon knew how to use them effectively. The Mi'kmaq also knew how to navigate coastal waters with their hardy canoes. By the time war erupted between that tribe and the British in the 1720s, the Mi'kmaq had learned to both seize and sail European vessels, creating a "Mi'kmaq Navy" of sorts. The Maliseet and Passamaquoddy maintained relations with tribes living deep within New England for centuries, utilizing a trail network that stretched for hundreds of kilometers. When conflict ignited in the late 1600s between the New England area tribes and the English, the Maliseet, Passamaquoddy, and later, the Mi'kmaq used this ancient trail system as a thoroughfare to attack advancing English settlements. France, the ally of all three Maritime First Nations, encouraged such attacks.

The Mi'kmaq
[McCord Museum MP – 0000.2027.2]

The Mi'kmaq, Maliseet, and Passamaquoddy became the scourge of the New England frontier. Armed with muskets, hatchets, and knives, these stealthy warriors kept the settlers of New England and, later, Nova Scotia, on edge. Although the dress of their warriors evolved over time (incorporating some European features) photographs taken in the nineteenth century show men in regalia not unlike those found in sketches and wood carvings going back to the time of King William's War in the late 1600s: headbands with vertical turkey or eagle feathers, long embroidered coats, leggings, and moccasins. While members of each of those tribes cooperated in most things (hunting communally, sharing their wealth, and making important political decisions by consensus), when it came to war, they fought on the battlefield as individuals, each man his own strategist. Sachems or chiefs were followed by the warriors only insofar as the individual bravery and wisdom of their leaders inspired confidence. Despite a legacy of valor, the First Nations paid an extraordinarily heavy price for their efforts during the colonial wars of the seventeenth and eighteenth centuries.

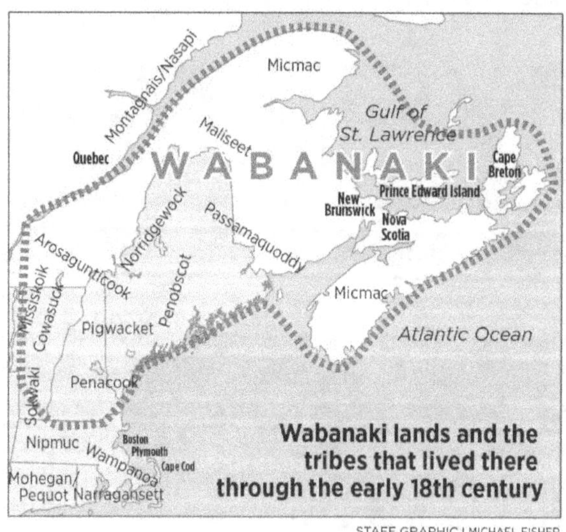

STAFF GRAPHIC | MICHAEL FISHER

Wabanahkik or Land of the Wabanaki

The primary European players in northeastern America, France, and Great Britain were no strangers to warfare. Out of the Dark Ages rode the feudal heavy cavalry that came to dominate the battlefields of

Europe during the age of chivalry (roughly the eleventh to the fifteenth centuries). French nobility excelled at producing such cavalry.

English "yeomen" armed with longbows demonstrated that heavy cavalry was vulnerable to soldiers who were not of noble birth. They smashed the mounted French knights at the battles of Crecy and Poitiers during the so-called Hundred Years' War (1337–1453). Such victories, along with the introduction of firearms into battle, led to the creation of professional royal armies drawn from the general population and taught to mass their firepower.

European military tactics were designed to deliver devastating blows to their similarly arrayed enemies with massed firepower, but these tactics, although well-suited to the open plains of Europe, proved problematic in forested America: the sniping from concealed positions that was characteristic of frontier warfare in America and the close hand-to-hand fighting that usually concluded an ambush were considered "unchivalrous" by many European generals. They resisted any training of their regular troops and militias in such methods. Yet European settlers who supplemented their diets with wild game and collected furs for domestic use and trade learned some of the lessons of forest warfare through such practices.

In order to survive, Europeans had to learn the skills of their First Nations allies and enemies as they pushed into the rugged backcountry of New England, New France (France's primary colony, with the fortress city of Québec as its capital), and the French colony in the Maritime region known as Acadia.

In 1710, the British seized the capital of Acadia, Port-Royal, and promptly renamed it Annapolis Royal in honor of the British monarch of the day. The British would receive several bloody surprises in the form of ambushes near Annapolis at the hands of First Nations warriors, but the First Nations could not match the military skills of Europeans at fortifying and laying siege to strategic places, employing artillery, and using naval forces to strike at multiple locations. Combined European and First Nations units became one of the most feared armed formations: First Nations warriors fought with great ferocity, and this trait merged with the technological prowess of Europeans to create a deadly hybrid force. Only the application of overwhelming counterforce by numerically superior European armies and navies was able to overcome this threat.

It was the seafaring powers of England, France, Spain, Portugal, and the Netherlands who struck out to explore the New World that was happened upon by Christopher Columbus in 1492. France and England, in particular, who were economic, military, and religious rivals in Europe, exported their rivalries to northeastern America. While the English explored and staked nominal claims to Maritime Canada, it was the eastern coast of what would eventually become the United States that really attracted their attention and first settlements. English Puritan towns and villages soon radiated out from the hub of English power, Boston, Massachusetts, founded in 1630. Although the Puritans were religious dissenters who rejected the state-sanctioned Church of England and its doctrines, they preferred nominal rule by the Crown of England especially given the enemies that surrounded them in America (France, Spain, and First Nations).

During the late 1600s, the tentacles of English settlement reached as far as the Kennebec River in present-day Maine. The Mi'kmaq, Maliseet, and Passamaquoddy became alarmed. They were allies of the French who had arrived to permanently settle in the Maritimes in the early 1600s. Having largely adopted Catholicism as their religion and having forged friendly relations with the French settlers who had peacefully occupied small tracts of land in Acadia, the tribes made common cause and lent some support to an uprising by First Nations in New England in 1675 through 1678. This firestorm known as King Philip's War or Metacom's Rebellion, after its main aboriginal protagonist, was a brutal affair. The war consumed numerous English settlements, some six hundred English lives and more than three thousand First Nations people killed or captured.

While the Mi'kmaq, Maliseet, and Passamaquoddy played only a minor role in Metacom's Rebellion, that terrible fight set the tone for poor relations between the English and First Nations during the coming decades in Acadia and, later, Nova Scotia. The tribes in Acadia recognized that the English settlers' hunger for First Nations' lands helped to spark the conflict and made note of alleged instances of English brutality and trickery, which characterized the uprising.

The type of warfare practiced by the European powers and their settlers with and against the First Nations was ruthless, involving scalping (i.e., removing the scalp or a portion of the crown of the head from an immobilized, wounded, or deceased enemy), the taking of hostages, and the torture of captives. Scalping had both European and North American origins. It was practiced extensively during the colonial wars from 1688 through 1760. Nova Scotia saw its share of French and British "bounties" paid for enemy scalps, including those of women and children. The colonial wars also saw their share of heroism, with accounts of First Nations warriors fighting to the death when surrounded by a numerically superior enemy force, stubborn captives determined to escape and see freedom, and a British brigadier general wading ashore under fire to help seize a French fortress.

Acadia was the focus of much unwanted attention from the warring European powers during the seventeenth and eighteenth centuries. It was a French colony with ill-defined boundaries that stretched well into Maine. It sat astride the sea approaches to both Québec and New England. It was rich in fish, furs, and agricultural produce. England challenged France's claim to the entire region but initially concentrated its efforts on coastal Maine. Acadia embraced not only the Mi'kmaq, Maliseet, and Passamaquoddy tribes, but the feared Penobscot Nation as well, established on the Maine waterway of the same name. Numerous smaller Abenaki tribes occupied the lands west of the Penobscot bordering New England. All of these tribes combined to form a pro-French Wabanaki Confederacy as a barrier to English expansion east from Massachusetts.

"Wabanaki" means "People of the Dawn," referring to the tribes who lived on the lands over which the sun first rose on the North American continent. These Wabanaki, linked by bonds of language and culture, formed an alliance whose chief goal was to oppose the advance of the English into Maine and Nova Scotia—their "Wabanahkik" or Land of the Wabanaki.

In 1710, the British captured Acadia, but in name only. France disputed the colony's boundaries and covertly supported First Nations opposing the British in the renamed colony of Nova Scotia. The French military and Catholic religious orders operated without regard for

British law in the territories now comprising New Brunswick, Maine, (east of the Kennebec River) and even interior mainland Nova Scotia.

The French

    The British presence in Nova Scotia, drawn principally from New England troops, traders, and fishers was a mere "toehold" within a ramshackle star-shaped fort at Annapolis and, later, a fortified fishing settlement at Canso. Both locations were neighbors to large numbers of French-speaking Acadian settlers whose loyalty to Great Britain was questionable. The fort and settlement at Annapolis became a British "island" in a "sea" of disinterested or openly hostile Acadians and First Nations. There was no Legislative Assembly. The British presence in the province was managed by a small governing council that sometimes displayed episodes of internal jealousy and infighting. British travel and trade were mainly by sea in order to avoid the dangerous land routes. In times of crisis, British forts were wholly reliant on the sea for resupply and reinforcement from Massachusetts—a colony that took a special interest in ensuring the survival of British Nova Scotia. The British regulars and New England militia who staffed the two English forts in the province remained on constant alert for a sudden attack. This was the state of affairs in Nova Scotia until the settlement of Halifax in 1749.

The British

Before 1710, the First Nations attention was largely focused on keeping New Englanders at bay along the Kennebec River frontier. After 1710, a British "cancer" appeared in their midst in the form of the British fort and settlement at Annapolis. Several attempts were made by the tribes to cut the "cancer" out. They very nearly succeeded. This effort did not end with the establishment of a new and powerful British military base at Halifax, but it became more difficult. A huge setback for First Nations came in the form of the French defeat at Fort Beauséjour on the Isthmus of Chignecto in 1755 and the final loss of the French fortress at Louisbourg on Cape Breton Island in 1758.

Beginning in 1755, thousands of Acadians would be summarily rounded up and expelled from Nova Scotia by the British.

Although the Mi'kmaq, Maliseet, and Passamaquoddy continued to fight after the fall of Louisbourg, their struggle came to an end through a combination of events: the Expulsion of their supporters, the Acadians; the British occupation of the lower St. John River; British "scorched earth" raids along both the St. John River and within the Mi'kmaq coastal homeland. Finally, with the British conquests of Québec (1759) and Montréal (1760), the First Nations sued for peace.

Abandoned by their French partners, the First Nations came into a final series of treaty and trade accommodations with the British at Halifax beginning in early 1760. While their wars with the colonial powers in northeastern America were at an end, faint thunder from these long-ago struggles still echo across battlefields at Annapolis, Grand-Pré, Beauséjour, Canso, Petitcodiac, Restigouche, and elsewhere.

This is an account of those struggles on the battlefields of "old" Nova Scotia.

CHAPTER 1
Setting the Stage

I am determined not to live until I have no country.

—Metacom, grand sachem of the
Wampanoag Confederacy of First Nations

July 1675. A full eclipse of the moon signaled to the New England tribes that the time was right to strike the English. Since the 1620 founding of the English Plymouth Colony in Massachusetts, tensions had been rising between local tribes and English settlers. Those settlers were pressing for more and more First Nations land sales and were attempting to impose English law on the autonomous tribes. The English had already fought and won an especially vicious war against the Pequot First Nation of New England in the late 1630s, driving that tribe to the edge of extinction. In the aftermath of the war, many English settlers developed a low opinion of First Nations generally, even with respect to tribes previously allied with them. One-time partners of the English, the Wampanoag, sensed the hostility and resolved to challenge these relative newcomers.

By the summer of 1675, the tribes had enough. Led by Metacom, the grand sachem or chief of the Wampanoag Alliance, the First Nations exploded in a series of attacks on scattered New England villages. Reduced by years of disease and fighting, the tribes still mounted an impressive effort against the settlements and their "garrison houses," or mini forts, driving back the poorly trained local militia. Only when the English utilized the skills of their remaining aboriginal allies (many "Christianized" First Nations) and developed the first "Ranger" units of settlers familiar with wilderness warfare did the initiative pass to the

English. One of the heroes of the English cause was Benjamin Church, who would later play an important role in the wars involving the French and First Nations in Acadia.

First Nations attacking a Garrison House, 1676

The French, who would first establish themselves in Acadia in 1605 and at Québec in 1608, pushed their colonial land claims to the edge of New England by the time of Metacom's Rebellion. They built religious missions and trading posts within Maine, east of the Kennebec River. French efforts to dominate the fur trade and their early alliance with the Algonquian-speaking First Nations put them at odds with the powerful Iroquois League, including the Mohawk First Nation and the league's sometime ally, England.

While tempted to aid the New England tribes at war with their European rival during the mid-1670s, French support proved to be minimal, mostly in the form of providing small amounts of gunpowder, ammunition, and foodstuffs. Also tempted to act on the side of the New England tribes were the Wabanaki Nations of which the Penobscot, Maliseet, and Mi'kmaq were the most powerful. Some western Abenaki tribes did join the fight and raided the English. The English eyed all the French-allied tribes with suspicion and apprehension: those First

Nations were mostly Catholic "papists"—considered natural enemies of the English Protestants of Massachusetts. The English saw the tribes as a cruel and barbaric enemy doing the bidding of France. Ironically, the Wabanaki tribes held the view that the slave-trading, witch-killing New Englanders were both cruel and barbaric. The Wabanaki had their own reasons for hating the English that had nothing to do with France.

Metacom and his allies ultimately succumbed to English power. The grand sachem was hunted down and killed by a party of rangers in 1676, his head mounted on a pike and displayed at the entrance to an English fort. His wife and child were sold into slavery. His supporters were scattered, destroyed, or forced into a punitive peace with the English. Their terrible fate was known to all the tribes in the northeast.

The Mi'kmaq became caught up on the fringes of the whirlwind that was Metacom's Rebellion. English seafaring raiders with a broad mandate to stop First Nations attacks on the New England frontier seized members of the Mi'kmaq tribe at Cape Sable, Nova Scotia, in late 1676. Many of those captured were sold into Caribbean slavery. The Mi'kmaq were known to the English as Cape Sable Indians, for it was in and around that western Nova Scotia location that New England fishers sometimes encountered the tribe. Before 1676, relations between the English and the Mi'kmaq were peaceful but not overly friendly.

The seizure prompted a retaliatory raid by the Mi'kmaq on New England fishers near Cape Sable the following summer. The raid was initially successful, but the captured fishers managed to turn the tables on some of the Mi'kmaq raiders, taking them as prisoners back to Massachusetts. The First Nations prisoners died at the hands of a frenzied mob. The initial English raid and the Mi'kmaq counterraid were ominous encounters that would soon be repeated when the kings and queens of Europe later elected to go to war. Their conflicts spilled over into their American colonies.

Metacom's Rebellion was the first war between the English and First Nations that saw captives taken out of New England. During that conflict, the captives were mostly carried to the French at Québec or Montréal in what was then popularly known as Canada (i.e., New France) and ransomed there, but in later wars, many captives would find their way to Acadia, especially along the Maliseet Trail from Maine to the Maliseet stockade at Meductic on the St. John River. The Maliseet were known to the English as St. John's Indians as that tribe resided all along the St. John River in Acadia. Some captives of the Maliseet were ransomed. Others were adopted by the tribe; a number were tortured or killed. A similar fate awaited Maliseet or other Wabanaki tribal members taken in battle by the English or seized by English raiders from the sea. English dungeons and slave plantations were the final destinations for many Wabanaki prisoners.

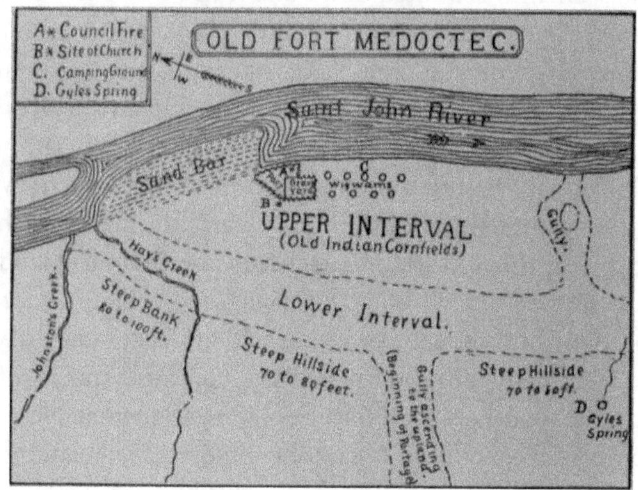

The Maliseet Fort at Meductic

Prior to the arrival of the French, the Mi'kmaq, Maliseet, and Passamaquoddy let the seasons dictate the nature and pace of their subsistent hunting, fishing, and gathering pursuits. Occasionally they warred on the Mohawk or fended off their ferocious raids. The Wabanaki tribes were avid moose hunters but gathered all the species of edible plants, fish, sea mammals, and fur-bearing animals available to them. Wood was a vital staple for their cooking fires, building their habitations (including the easily transportable wigwam), and their canoes, weapons, and crafts, but the arrival of Europeans and the acquisition of firearms changed the First Nations way of life. They went from stockpiling necessities to securing an abundance of furs in order to trade, mainly with the French. Some First Nations members congregated at the newly established French mission settlements while others remained at traditional sites. In many instances, these places were one and the same.

Most Wabanaki maintained their migratory, aboriginal ways, incorporating European technologies into their daily lives only insofar as they were useful. Spring and summer still saw them congregate near major water resources while fall and winter saw the tribes break into smaller "bands" bent on pursuing big game like the moose into the interior. Trade also brought them into contact and sometimes rivalry with the Iroquois and English. Skills learned as hunter/gatherers and part-time warriors were soon honed into full-time employment in the fur trade as economic "middlemen" between other tribes and the French and as a hardened militia inclined to help France.

As early as 1609, French Catholic missionaries, most notably Jesuit priests, were established in Acadia, first on the Penobscot River and, later, at Port-Royal. Franciscan priests established a mission at Meductic, which they later abandoned around the dawn of the eighteenth century, but the Jesuits quickly reestablished that mission in 1701. Catholic religious orders also put down roots on the eastern Acadian coast, on Cape Breton Island and at Shubenacadie in the interior of Nova Scotia. The Wabanaki were soon among Catholicism's strongest converts. French clerics found ways to make Catholic teachings consistent with First Nations spirituality and traditional practices. On the other hand, the Spanish and the English demanded that indigenous peoples under their control both assimilate and adopt European religious beliefs and practices. Intermarriage between the French and First Nations helped to establish and solidify strong ties of blood and culture while the English tended to keep the First Nations at arm's length. The Spanish engaged in the wholesale slaughter of aboriginal peoples in many of their colonies.

While some priests played the role of mediator with the advancing English and, after 1710, with the British occupiers of Nova Scotia, other notable clerics encouraged and even accompanied First Nations warriors on raids against New England and Nova Scotia forts and settlements from the 1680s into the 1750s. Fathers Rale, Gaulin, Le Loutre, and Maillard would all lend both spiritual and temporal support to the Wabanaki fighters. The Catholic missions, established on the major river systems of Acadia, served both religious and strategic military purposes, gathering together First Nations families for religious instruction and easy resupply by the French Crown of a ready-made strike force. Control of the rivers meant control of the region.

New England militias became more proficient during Metacom's Rebellion, especially with the development and deployment of ranger units. New England was largely left to its own devices during that conflict, unsupported by ambivalent, even mildly hostile, royal and colonial governments (i.e., England, Virginia, New York, etc.). The New England governments were forced to rely on one another for support given the scope and ferocity of the First Nations attacks. They closed ranks, abandoned indefensible towns, shortened their battle lines, and received resupply from the sea. Starved for powder and shot and pressed by English raiding parties who burned their crops, destroyed their winter supplies, and laid waste to their villages, the First Nations war effort collapsed. The rebellious tribes were punished severely for their uprising, losing land, freedom, and sometimes their lives.

The Mi'kmaq, Maliseet, and Passamaquoddy learned from the failure of Metacom's Rebellion that a close alliance with France was in their best interest. While the English might offer cheap and more durable trade goods, they seemed ravenous for First Nations lands and were vehemently anti-Catholic. The Wabanaki tribes knew that a fight was coming and prepared accordingly.

The French capital of Port-Royal was attacked six times and occupied several times by the English before it finally fell into British hands for the last time after a siege in 1710. The First Nations in Acadia remained firmly in the French interest during all of that period.

A decade after Metacom's Rebellion, war clouds appeared on the horizon once more.

The newly appointed royal governor of all New England, Sir Edmund Andros, struck First Nations settlements in western Maine in early 1688 in response to renewed Abenaki raids. He also struck at the trading establishment of one Jean-Vincent d'Abbadie de Saint-Castin on Penobscot Bay. Saint-Castin was a French baron and soldier born at Escout in Bearn, France, in 1652. He came to New France at an early age and immersed himself in the Wabanaki way of life while serving with the military in Acadia. He married one First Nations woman, then another, and had several métis children, including at least two sons, Bernard-Anselme and Joseph. He used his First Nations family, commercial and military ties to gather the Abenaki and Penobscot to the French cause and challenge English claims to coastal Maine beginning in 1667. Considering the baron a French promoter of First Nations raids on the New England frontier, Andros had the baron's home sacked, but his prey escaped. This raid, in close proximity to the Maliseet and Passamaquoddy homelands and targeting an individual whom they considered one of their own, enraged the tribes. A new conflict erupted that would bring the Maliseet, Mi'kmaq, and Passamaquoddy to the center stage of the fight for possession of northeastern America.

CHAPTER 2
King William's War

Spanish civilization crushed the Indian, English civilization scorned and neglected him, French civilization embraced and cherished him.

—Author Francis Parkman,
renowned student of the colonial wars in America

September 1696. Vengeance. Taking vengeance was certainly on the minds and in the hearts of some three hundred New England men and one hundred of their First Nations allies as they arrived offshore of the sleepy Acadian village of Beaubassin. With memories of loved ones scalped, burned alive, or carried off from the ruined hamlets of New England, this force had no room for mercy in their plans.

Located on the windswept Tantramar Marshes near present-day Amherst, Nova Scotia, Beaubassin, a village established by the French in 1672, was a farming community. It was not fortified to any meaningful degree. As the Acadian militia and local Mi'kmaq warriors were called out to defend the twenty or more Acadian homes, barns, and chapels, they must have known it would be a difficult fight.

Since 1688, the First Nations of Acadia, supported by the French, had been delivering a series of hammerblows against the New England frontier settlements. Their crowning achievement was the capture and destruction of New England's Fort William Henry at Pemaquid, Maine, in the summer of 1696. This strong stone fort was reduced by five hundred Wabanaki warriors and French cannons. It was probably the most impressive French and First Nations victory in what came to be known as King William's War (1688–1697). The Acadians of Beaubassin celebrated the French victory by posting a proclamation of the event on the door of their local chapel. It proved to be a serious mistake.

It was payback time. The New England force lying offshore in Chignecto Bay was led by Maj. Benjamin Church, a militia leader and ranger with a long history of fighting the First Nations in and around Massachusetts. The tribes lying east of that colony had come to be known collectively to the English as the Eastern Indians. To the English way of thinking, French instigators were to blame for the brutal First Nations attacks against their settlements. The most accessible French men, women, and children were the Acadians who diked and farmed the marshes of the Tantramar.

Hell would be unleashed on those farmers.

Although Major Church's landing was opposed by the Acadians and First Nations warriors, he managed to get his troops ashore and into Beaubassin. He lost several men in the effort. Nine days of mayhem followed. Church was infuriated by the proclamation found nailed to the chapel door celebrating the success of French arms. Buildings were looted and burned. Inhabitants were killed. Livestock was slaughtered. Church vowed to return and decimate the village and surrounding area to an even greater degree if the towns of New England continued to suffer under French and First Nations attacks.

Col. Benjamin Church

One of the most prosperous villages in all Acadia had now met the same terrible fate as English settlements at Falmouth (now Portland, Maine), Salmon Falls, York, Wells, Dover, and Pemaquid.

This was not Benjamin Church's first visit to Acadia nor would it be his last. Born in 1639 in Massachusetts Plymouth Colony, this hero of the Great Swamp Fight during Metacom's Rebellion raided along the Maine coast of Acadia early in King William's War. He fought the First Nations opposing the English settlement of Falmouth, Maine, in 1689, losing twenty men. While initially successful, he left the settlers of Fort Loyal at Falmouth Neck alone and relatively unprotected while his forces withdrew to Boston. The result was a devastating defeat when four hundred to five hundred French, Mi'kmaq, Maliseet, and other Wabanaki warriors under the leadership of French commander Joseph-Francois Hertel de la Fresnière and the Baron Saint-Castin appeared in May 1690 and forced the surrender of the fort. They killed two hundred English and took over one hundred prisoners. Many of the prisoners, including one James Alexander, found their way into captivity at the Maliseet fort at Meductic. Church returned later that summer and was forced to bury the piles of dead settlers at Falmouth.

In October 1696, after his descent on Beaubassin, Church helped to lead a four-hundred-man force against the French stronghold of Fort Nashwaak (sometimes called Fort St. Joseph) on the banks of the St. John River opposite present-day Fredericton, New Brunswick. Fort Nashwaak was, at that time, capital of all Acadia. It was a four-sided bastion of wooden palisades erected in 1691 not far from the Maliseet village at Meductic. First Nations from both Maine and the Maritimes gathered at Nashwaak to feast, counsel, and be supplied by the French. It was from Nashwaak that the devastating Wabanaki attacks on the New England frontier settlements were frequently launched. To the English, Nashwaak was a "hornet's nest" that had to be dealt with.

Forewarned by scouts of the seaborne approach of the English at the mouth of the St. John River, the French, joined by Maliseet First Nation warriors, fought a rearguard action, first at Nerepis, then finally concentrating their forces at Nashwaak. The English, led by Col. John Hathorne and accompanied by Major Church arrived near the French fort in four armed sloops (moderately sized vessels) and set about on a two-day siege of Fort Nashwaak, beginning October 18, 1696.

English cannons were landed south of the nearby Nashwaak River, a tributary of the St. John River, and earthworks were erected. French and Maliseet raiders struck English troops advancing along the south bank of the Nashwaak. The English bombardment was largely ineffective and was countered by the guns of the fort. Acadian privateers, settlers, and the Maliseet added to the garrison's intense fire. The French were reinforced, and one English cannon was put out of action. The English were finally driven off. They retreated down the St. John River pursued by the French and First Nations warriors. The New England force had suffered eight killed and seventeen wounded; French casualties were reported as one killed and two wounded.

France's answer to Maj. Benjamin Church was its governor in Acadia, Joseph Robineau de Villebon. Born at Québec in 1655, he was educated in France. He became that Colony's governor by default when the serving governor at Port-Royal, de Meneval, was carried off by English raiders. Villebon was called upon to revive flagging French fortunes in the region after 1690. Like his ardent supporter, Louis de Baude, Comte de Frontenac, governor-general of New France at Québec, Villebon was determined to go on the offensive against the English. He rallied the Wabanaki tribes from his base at Nashwaak and devastated the New England frontier from the east. Frontenac struck at the English and their Iroquois allies from the north: New York and New England towns like Schenectady and Haverhill (just north of Boston) were razed by forces at Frontenac's direction.

Villebon was forced to revive the French war effort after the English successfully attacked Acadia's capital, Port-Royal, in May 1690. Led by Sir William Phips, a sometime shipbuilder, treasure hunter, and military man, a makeshift English naval force of seven warships and nearly five hundred militiamen caught the French fort at Port-Royal in a state of rebuilding and disarray. Cannons that could have blunted the English assault were not in their firing positions, and the garrison was undermanned. There were less than twenty muskets in the entire fort. Surrender was almost immediate.

The aftermath of the surrender foreshadowed events at Beaubassin. Alleging that the surrendering French had violated the terms of their capitulation, the town was plundered, livestock slaughtered, and religious places desecrated by the English. In the aftermath of Port-Royal's fall, Villebon, who was not on hand for the tragedy, moved Acadia's capital to the St. John River, first to Jemseg and then farther up the river to Nashwaak.

Emboldened by his almost painless capture of Port-Royal, Sir William Phips set out to repeat his success by attacking Québec in October 1690. He failed. His ships were pounded by French cannons high atop the imposing cliffs of Québec, and he was forced to retreat. The aging Count Frontenac reportedly declared in response to a call for Québec's surrender, "I have no reply to make to your general other than from the mouths of my cannons and muskets."

Frontenac, like Villebon, was a "true" war governor. He was a close friend and ally of the Algonquian-speaking tribes he relied on to defend the borders of New France and its dependencies. While New England alone boasted nearly one hundred thousand inhabitants at the time of King William's War, New France had fewer than fifteen thousand residents and Acadia only one thousand. Yet this imbalance in population did not translate into an imbalance in military effort or success. Both Acadia and New France could rely on nature and geography as allies. Winter made the sea approaches to those colonies dangerous due to rough seas and ice. Tucked up behind a formidable stockade of rocks, lakes, and forests, the French colonies were only vulnerable during three seasons of the year, mainly from the ocean side. The protecting forests were inhabited by friendly First Nations warriors schooled in woodcraft and ready to raise the hatchet in defense of their Catholic allies. The fur trade and colonial wars forged a French militia and leadership that understood frontier warfare and the need for good relations with their First Nations allies. These "coureur des bois", coupled with the Wabanaki, Huron, Ottawa, and other pro-French tribes created a martial mix that the freedom-loving, but self-interested and rarely cooperative English colonists had a difficult time matching.

The French soon discovered from their First Nations allies how to survive in the wilderness and fight during all seasons. The French military had been bred in a European tradition that saw campaigns usually end when the weather turned cold. English rangers like Benjamin Church and his men learned similar forest warfare and survival techniques, yet British regular forces and New England militia tended to cling to the European style of training and troop deployments, moving, marching, and fighting in long lines of infantry. They would pay a heavy price for their failure to adapt during the colonial wars with the French.

The Mi'kmaq, Maliseet, and Passamaquoddy First Nations were especially active during King William's War. The European theater of war originated when the so-called Glorious Revolution of 1688 deposed Catholic King James II of England in favor of Protestant King William and his wife, Mary, who ruled as coregents. William and Mary's support swung England behind the Protestant powers on the European continent already at war with France, but in America, war between the French and English had already begun prompted, in part, by Governor Andros's raid on the home of Baron Saint-Castin in early 1688.

The English raided the French fort of St. Louis at Guysborough, Nova Scotia, in early 1690 as part of Sir William Phips effort to capture Acadia. A dozen French soldiers held off eighty raiders for six hours until firebombs burned the place to the ground. Capt. John Alden, a descendant of famous Pilgrim parents who arrived in Massachusetts aboard the ship *Mayflower* in 1620, was also dispatched by Phips to raid Cape Sable, Grand-Pré, and Chignecto.

The Mi'kmaq and Maliseet were in the service of France, attacking Salmon Falls in present-day Maine in March 1690, followed by the assault on Fort Loyal. The Salmon Falls settlement was destroyed with thirty English killed and nearly twice that number captured. They also hit York and Wells in Maine in 1692. Led by the Penobscot sachem Madocawando, father-in-law to Baron Saint-Castin, more than 180 New Englanders were killed and captured at York alone during the infamous Candlemas raid in January 1692. Many of the captured were later ransomed on a mission to Québec by Capt. John Alden. The Maliseet were also in action at Oyster River, New Hampshire, in July 1694. This complex attack led by Commander de Villieu for the French and the leadership of the Wabanaki, including Madocawando, saw two separate forces rendezvous and then devastate the Oyster River Plantation deep within New England. The Maliseet element of this strike force would have had to travel over five hundred kilometers (more than three hundred miles) along overland trails, by canoe, and across portage routes in order to reach their final objective. More than one hundred English died in the subsequent attack while less than thirty were taken as prisoners. Both tribes participated in the combined French and First Nations assault by land and sea that forced the surrender of Fort William Henry at Pemaquid in 1696.

Madocawando was born in 1630 and became leader of the Penobscot First Nation some time before Metacom's Rebellion. There is an indication that he was also considered chief sachem of the Maliseet Nation, as well, for a time. He began to vigorously attack the English after his daughter's husband, Baron Saint-Castin, was the object of Governor Andros's raid in 1688. Madocawando was renowned for his courage in battle and hatred of the English, but it was not beneath him to negotiate with his enemies toward a just peace. His objectives for his people did not simply mimic the goals of Saint-Castin or the French.

A woodcut of the First Nations Attack on Dover, New Hampshire, 1689

The English had long sought to push their colonial frontier beyond Casco Bay, even beyond the Kennebec River, east, and deeper into Maine. They established themselves at Pemaquid on the coast, just west of Penobscot. This site drove an English wedge between eastern and western Wabanaki communications and trade. A wooden stockade that the English built there in 1677 was destroyed by a First Nations force led by Baron Saint-Castin in 1689. The English rebuilt the place as a stone fortress with walls in some places twenty feet high and six feet thick and deployed upward of twenty cannons to protect the place. Fort William Henry was the largest and most expensive fortress in the region.

The First Nations hated the new fort at Pemaquid, and the French resolved to destroy it. In 1696 the French military hero, Pierre Le Moyne d'Iberville, with four warships and a force of Mi'kmaq warriors, met Baron Saint-Castin and a Wabanaki war party at Penobscot, moving quickly to isolate the English fortress. A two-day siege followed. French mortars pounded the fort, and the First Nations menaced its ramparts. The English commander was Pasco Chubb, a man hated by the attacking Wabanaki for past transgressions. He was in charge of a nervous garrison and, fearing a sudden collapse, surrendered on terms that allowed for an eventual prisoner exchange. The French destroyed the fortress walls with gunpowder and burned its buildings. The English frontier east of Casco Bay evaporated. The French and Wabanaki had blunted the English advance for the time being.

A reconstruction of the English Fort at Pemaquid, Maine

The Mi'kmaq later defended against the English retaliatory strike at Beaubassin, and the Maliseet fought to defend the stockade at Nashwaak when the English attacked. The Mi'kmaq and French laid waste to virtually every English settlement in Newfoundland in a spectacular campaign in late 1696 and early 1697.

King William's War ended with the Treaty of Ryswick in September 1697. The war resulted in a virtual "draw" among the European powers involved, and in America, colonial boundaries did not change. King William's War proved to be only an interlude before Queen Anne's War (1702–1713), which would have a much more profound impact on the French, English, and First Nations positions in the northeast.

King William's War demonstrated the tactical benefit of close cooperation between First Nations forces, colonial militia, and naval forces. This combination worked well for the French at Pemaquid and the English at Beaubassin, but the war also revealed the worst wartime traits of the combatants: Benjamin Church was infamous as a killer of First Nations captives, including women and children; Capt. Pasco Chubb, late commander of Fort William Henry at Pemaquid, once feigned a parley under a flag of truce in order to kill unarmed Wabanaki sachems. This trickery ended in a bloody free-for-all of hand-to-hand fighting with one warrior seizing a musket from an English soldier and using it to bayonet three of his surrounding attackers. This allowed

Taxous, one of the sachems, to flee. Madocawando, the Penobscot leader, may have been among those killed at Chubb's direction, but the record is unclear. Maj. Richard Waldron used similar tactics in order to kill and enslave a large party of local Abenaki in 1676. He was singled out for especially harsh treatment when a joint Abenaki and Maliseet force raided Dover, New Hampshire, in June 1689. Meantime, French and Wabanaki forces, sometimes accompanied by priests, gave "no quarter" when they raided Kittery, Maine, and returned to the vicinity of Wells and Pemaquid in 1697.

The Baron Saint – Castin

By the peace of 1697, the "status quo" was restored, and the First Nations were left unsupported. The tribes in close proximity to New England made peace in January 1699. The Mi'kmaq, Maliseet, and Passamaquoddy scorned any peace and sharpened their knives and hatchets for the next round of fighting. Those tribes had profited not only from the plunder of English settlements but from the flow of captives coming their way from New England.

John Gyles, a young boy of nine, taken by the Maliseet when Pemaquid was first attacked in 1689, represented a typical captive. His father was killed and his brother carried off to Penobscot when the First Nations struck. John was taken by way of the Maliseet Trail to the tribe's stronghold at Meductic on the river St. John, where he served at hard labor, but he also learned to live off the forest and was taught the language of the tribe. Other English captives, such as James Alexander of Falmouth, shared Gyles captivity. Alexander's fate is not known. In 1695, Gyles was sold to an Acadian and eventually repatriated at war's end. He later wrote a valuable account of his captivity and served the English as an interpreter of First Nations dialects, a trading post manager, and a military man. He would sail with Benjamin Church back to Acadia during Queen Anne's War.

Québec had survived the English siege of 1690. Acadia was fully restored to the French from its nominal capture. Growing Acadian settlements formed something of an "arc of prosperity" from Port-Royal, round the Bay of Fundy, to Chignecto, and into the river valleys of what is today southeastern New Brunswick. The St. John River too had a small Acadian population. The French were careful not to encroach upon or antagonize their Wabanaki neighbors. Not adverse to commerce with New Englanders who plied local waters in trading vessels, the Acadian settlers still remained wary of any English who might suddenly attack, burn their homes, scalp their neighbors, and loot their chapels. This brutal form of warfare would be revisited on the Acadians during Queen Anne's War.

And the worst was yet to come.

CHAPTER 3
Queen Anne's War

The Queen of Great Britain's Arms were superior to those of the King of France and he had surrendered up Newfoundland and the land on this side; to which [the First Nations Delegates] replyed, the French never said anything to us about it and we wonder how they would give it away without asking us, God having at first placed us there and They having nothing to do to give it away.

—English Commissioners recording a treaty with the Eastern Indians, Portsmouth, New Hampshire, July 1713

August 1703. Alexandre Leneuf de la Vallière de Beaubassin was in command of a mixed force of French, Mi'kmaq, and Kennebec Abenaki, lying silently in wait in the forests of Maine. Alongside him was a French Jesuit priest, Sébastien Rale, mentor to the Abenaki. Born in June 1666, in New France, Beaubassin hailed from a family who had received a land grant from the French Crown, embracing a Chignecto settlement in Acadia bearing his family's name. It was, of course, the same settlement destroyed by Benjamin Church's vengeful raiders in 1696, but revenge is a two-edged sword.

After his force was blessed by the Jesuit, Beaubassin divided his men into six units and then struck six English settlements simultaneously: Cape Porpoise, Saco, Scarborough, Spurwink, Cape Elizabeth, and Casco. The destruction was terrible. Only the strongest English defenses survived. Beaubassin and his forces are said to have laid waste to more than eighty kilometers of English territory and killed or captured more than three hundred of the enemy. War had been opened once again on the New England frontier. A fire that started on the battlefields of

Europe in July 1701 spread to the forests of America. Known as the War of the Spanish Succession in Europe, it was Queen Anne's War in America. While in Europe, the Great Powers fought over who would succeed Charles II on the Spanish Throne, in America, the conflict was designed to settle religious, economic, and territorial claims and determine which of the expanding colonial empires of France, Spain, or England would dominate the continent.

A French priest prays for French and First Nations raiders

In order to retaliate for the French and First Nations raids that ignited the American conflict, New England once again turned to Benjamin Church. He struck out by sea toward Acadia in May 1704 with three warships and fourteen other transports. Thoughts of the recent notorious French and First Nations raid on Deerfield, Massachusetts, in February 1704 were probably on his mind. Fifty French soldiers, a mix of regulars and militia, accompanied by three hundred Abenaki, Mohawk, Wyandot, and Pocumtuc First Nations warriors set out on this winter raid from Canada. More than fifty English settlers were surprised and killed, with pursuing forces being ambushed and badly punished by the raiders. More than one hundred English settlers were taken captive. The unfortunate prisoners were marched off in the winter snow for a month-long trek into captivity in New France. The French and First Nations war party lost eleven killed and twenty-two wounded. The Wabanaki, in turn, revisited York and Wells in Maine with raids in the spring of 1704.

The Raid on Deerfield, Massachusetts, 1704

Benjamin Church had been commissioned a colonel by Massachusetts governor Joseph Dudley for a retaliatory strike on Acadia. With a combined force of five hundred militia and allied First Nations warriors, Church once again raided the Acadian coast of Maine, attacking Saint-Castin's trading post at Penobscot, seizing the daughter of his foe and grandchildren (the baron being absent in France). He next raided a mixed French and Passamaquoddy village near present-day St. Stephen, New Brunswick, destroying dwellings and killing or capturing more than 30 inhabitants. Then it was off to Grand-Pré. Like Beaubassin in King William's War, Grand-Pré was a largely prosperous unfortified farming community of some five hundred souls on the Minas Basin in Acadia. Also like Beaubassin, Grand-Pré consisted of considerable marshlands diked by the Acadians. Although the Acadians played no part in the Deerfield raid, they were earmarked by New England to pay the price for the French success. Colonel Church was under orders to secure Acadian prisoners who could then be exchanged for the Deerfield captives. Church would spend three days picking the Grand-Pré settlement apart.

Church's force arrived in the Minas Basin in mid-June 1704. Taking advantage of a forested island that screened their movements, Church's force advanced into a position from which their colonel could send a flag of truce into the Grand-Pré settlement, demanding its immediate surrender. Lt. John Gyles, former captive of the Maliseet, carried the written demand. Rather than surrender, the Acadians and local Mi'kmaq found time to evacuate the town. Acadian militia and Mi'kmaq warriors returned to Grand-Pré to snipe at the English. The English, in turn, unleashed a cannon filled with grapeshot at the defenders. Grapeshot is a lethal mix of metal balls, slugs, or other assorted metal pieces. The militia and First Nations warriors withdrew.

The English raiders pushed into the town the next day, destroying sixty homes, mills, barns, and killing seventy cattle. Skirmishes produced a small number of casualties on each side. That night the English raiders fortified themselves behind a makeshift bastion of logs in the middle of Grand-Pré. On day three, Church ordered the Acadian dikes destroyed. Years of hard work were demolished in a few hours. The Acadians' remaining harvest was also destroyed as the English seemingly withdrew, but the raiders struck back at returning inhabitants as they came to salvage any remains. Colonel Church finally set off for the Acadian settlement at Pisiquit, Minas Basin (near present-day Windsor, Nova Scotia) where nearly fifty prisoners were seized. Casualties on both sides for the raids on the Minas settlements were around a dozen in total.

Colonel Church and his force sailed to Port-Royal after their attack on Pisiquit but accomplished little there. They may have found the French fortifications too imposing, but some reports claimed that Governor Dudley ordered Church not to strike that center of an illicit, but profitable, trade between New England and the French. Stymied at the capital of Acadia, Church decided to return to Beaubassin. This time the colonel's prior activities in the region had alerted the inhabitants of that place to English intentions. They evacuated to the forest with their prized possessions. Church came ashore, and his force skirmished with the inhabitants hiding in the forest. The English burned forty abandoned homes and barns and killed the livestock. Finally, he set out for Boston with his prisoners in tow.

The idea that raids by the French and Wabanaki First Nations could be diminished if the English captured Port-Royal was popular during Queen Anne's War. New England was also keen to stop French privateers who used Port-Royal as a base to decimate their fishing fleet. The French fort at Port-Royal, built on the remnants of previous fortifications at that site, was constructed in the "Vauban" style with sloped earthworks, ditches, and surrounded by a log palisade and obstacles. The site proved to be one of the most frequently attacked fortifications in North American history. Two attempts were made in 1707 alone to capture this capital of Acadia. Both failed. The first was an eleven-day siege in June 1707. The effort was not insignificant. More than one thousand colonial militia backed by New England First Nations warriors were enrolled for the attempt, supported by twenty-four ships of the Royal Navy. John Gyles once again saw himself enlisted as a witness to history, serving in the ranks as a translator. The French at Port-Royal had reinforced both the structures and manpower at their fort. France's famous Troupes de la Marine, regular naval troops, had 150 men in place. Saint-Castin's métis son, Bernard-Anselme, arrived with one hundred Wabanaki warriors. Acadian militia represented a further sixty men.

The English landed forces both north and south of the fort in an effort to begin a formal siege. A French attempt at an ambush failed, and the forces involved retired to Port-Royal. Still the French governor Daniel d'Auger de Subercase resolved to keep the English attackers off balance. His men harassed the besiegers. Rumors spread among the English that French reinforcements were on the way. A dispute broke out among English commanders over the safety of landing the English artillery. The English made a final futile attempt to storm the fort, then packed up, and sailed away. English casualties were light. The defenders lost sixteen killed and as many wounded.

Recriminations followed. The English commander of the Port-Royal expedition John March was ordered to hold in place at Casco Bay, and reinforcements were sent to him, but March resigned in favor of his second-in-command, Francis Wainwright, and many of the men deserted. Still the English fleet made it back to Port-Royal on August

21, 1707, and troops went ashore once again. The French had made additional preparations outside of the walls of their fort and drove the English back. After the English finally made camp, a woodcutting party was successfully ambushed by a French and First Nations force, killing nine English. The English retreated again, and the rumors suggested that they were surrounded by swarms of French and Wabanaki.

The English tried in desperation to surprise the French, landing a second time at a different location. A hot fight ensued, hand-to-hand, and the English were driven back. The English gave up the effort on September 1 and sailed off. More than twenty English were reportedly killed, but the French put that number much higher, at nearly two hundred. The French and Wabanaki irregular forces seem to have borne the brunt of the casualties on the defenders' side, but the numbers were small (five killed and three times as many wounded).

If nothing else, the New Englanders were persistent. Despite infighting at the highest levels of their colonial governments, a new plan finally found favor with Queen Anne, and she dispatched ships and men to assist, led by Gen. Francis Nicholson. Nicholson was a soldier who had served in a number of colonial administrations and commanded an ill-fated expedition by land from New York to capture New France. Now he was ordered to take Port-Royal.

1710 would be the decisive year.

Just as in King William's War, English captives flowed to Canada and Acadia during Queen Anne's War. The Deerfield raid in 1704 produced many including seven-year-old Eunice Williams. Her six-year-old sister and a younger brother were both killed in the raid, and her parents and remaining siblings were made captive. Her mother was later killed by a Mohawk warrior during the terrible winter march to New France. The Kahnawake Mohawk, unlike their fellow Iroquois, were Catholic converts allied with the French. Eunice was adopted by a Mohawk family, converted to Catholicism (her father having been a Puritan minister), married a Mohawk man, bore mixed-race children, and except for brief periods in her life, remained at Kahnawake. In fact, over thirty children and young adults were adopted into the raiding tribes and were never repatriated. Only 89 out of 109 captives even survived the trek to Canada, but out of those who did survive, most of the adults were redeemed by late 1706 through a combination of ransom and prisoner exchanges, some involving the Minas Acadians taken by Church.

Other captives were more resistant to their predicament: Hannah Dunston, a young Puritan mother taken captive during King William's War in an Abenaki raid on Haverhill, Massachusetts (1697), is said to have killed and scalped ten of her Abenaki captors with the help of two other captives. They then made good their escape in the canoes of the First Nations raiders.

After the aborted sieges of 1707, Subercase, governor of Acadia, took steps to prepare for what would be the inevitable "third try" by the English. Trees were cleared to improve lines of sight, and buildings were bomb-proofed, but his three hundred troops were about to face a British force of more than two thousand regulars, militia, and Iroquois warriors, supported by the Royal Navy. In October 1710, the British arrived off Port-Royal. One of their transports, the *Caesar*, ran aground attempting to navigate the Annapolis River, with the loss of its captain, some crew, and twenty-five soldiers, with others managing to reach shore, but this was the last major English tragedy of the campaign. English forces began landing on October 6. Early skirmishing did not deter the English from establishing their main camp and commencing siege operations. One of those who schooled the attacking force in siege warfare tactics was a young officer, Paul Mascarene. English naval fire smashed into the fort. When English siege cannons came ashore and were brought within three hundred feet of the ramparts, it was time to surrender. A capitulation was negotiated.

The garrison was allowed to depart for France. The local Acadians were promised protection, provided they swore an oath of allegiance to the British Crown. On October 16, 1710, the English took formal possession of Port-Royal, changing its name to Annapolis Royal in honor of Queen Anne. The French fort was now called Fort Anne. Samuel Vetch, a businessman and lobbyist with high-level ties in London, was named the first British governor at Annapolis Royal in the renamed colony of Nova Scotia. Vetch, who commanded some forces during the siege had been involved with the illegal trade between Port-Royal and New England before the attack.

The Acadian settlers in the nearby area remained calm, no doubt hoping for a swift return of French forces. The Mi'kmaq, Maliseet, and Passamaquoddy refused to accept the British presence and soon found ways to oppose it. France plotted its ultimate return but, in the meantime, encouraged the First Nations to keep the English "bottled up" at Annapolis.

In 1711, the young métis Baron Saint-Castin, Bernard-Anselme, was given a commission by France to oversee First Nations relations and command troops. He and a mixed Abenaki and Mi'kmaq force saw an opportunity to deal the English a blow in June 1711 at a place soon to be called "Bloody Creek" along the Annapolis River at Carleton Corner, Nova Scotia.

The garrison of British regulars and New England militia stationed at the former French fort at Port-Royal (Fort Anne) passed a hard winter during 1710–1711, reducing their effectiveness. Supplies were low, and local Acadians were reluctant to be seen provisioning the occupiers. Timber was needed to repair the fort, but Acadian cooperation for any logging venture was minimal, and British teams sent out to cut timber were harassed by French and First Nations raiding parties skulking in the vicinity. In an effort to overawe the local inhabitants and keep the raiders at bay, Samuel Vetch dispatched a force of seventy New England militiamen on an expedition up the Annapolis River. Around fifty to one hundred French and First Nations warriors were recently arrived to oppose any British move.

On June 21, 1711, the English force went up the river in small boats. The French and First Nations, alerted to the English advance, set up an ambush at a site were a creek empties into the river. Divided into two groups, the lead English crew rowed into the ambush. All but one of the English died. Although caution should have dictated that the second group of English troops approach the area with care after hearing gunfire, they did not. They too were ambushed, surrounded, cut down, and the survivors forced to surrender. None escaped. A disciplined, European-trained force had been beaten by the warriors of the Acadian forest.

The British defeat was a signal for a more general uprising although many local Acadian families simply departed the area. A force of six hundred Acadians, Abenaki, and Mi'kmaq laid siege to Fort Anne under the joint leadership of Saint-Castin and a priest, Antoine Gaulin, but without artillery, the attackers could do little. Fort Anne could be resupplied from the sea, and significant reinforcements soon arrived. The attackers fled.

The Mi'kmaq, Maliseet, Passamaquoddy, and other Wabanaki continued to raid the New England settlements for the remainder of Queen Anne's War, including the frequently attacked English settlements at York and Wells, Maine, in 1712 (killing or capturing almost one thousand New Englanders during the course of the entire conflict), but increasingly, Nova Scotia became the principal battleground. The Mi'kmaq were not inclined to make peace with the British. They raided the new English fishing settlement established at Port Roseway (present-day Shelburne, Nova Scotia) in July 1715 and set it ablaze, utterly destroying it. In response, the English launched raids on the Acadian settlements at Canso and Chedabucto (Guysborough, Nova Scotia) in a weeklong endeavor in 1718. They destroyed a fort, plundered villages, and captured ships. These were the first tentative efforts by the British to subjugate the restless Acadians and First Nations in Nova Scotia beyond Annapolis.

Queen Anne's War ended in 1713 with the Treaty of Utrecht, which was actually a series of treaties signed among the European combatants in March and April 1713. France and England agreed by the terms of the treaty that France would give up all its North American territories where British arms had been marginally successful: Newfoundland, the Hudson Bay posts, and Acadia. Yet the boundaries of Acadia were not defined with any precision. Prior to 1713, the French had claimed that Acadia included all mainland Nova Scotia, present-day New Brunswick, and most of Maine to the banks of the Kennebec River. After 1713, France would only concede that Acadia consisted of the area around Annapolis.

The Wabanaki First Nations were not parties to the Utrecht agreements and, technically speaking, remained in a state of war (or rebellion, depending on one's view of their status) with the English. Mi'kmaq and Maliseet lands, France insisted, were beyond French jurisdiction, yet France retained control over Isle Saint-Jean (Prince Edward Island) and Isle Royale (Cape Breton Island). On Isle Royale, they started construction of an impressive fortress and town at Louisbourg. This fortress would protect French rights to the fishery, guard the sea-lanes to Québec, provide a trading and resupply base for the Acadians and First Nations, and help hold Maine and New Brunswick in the French orbit. It was also a convenient privateer base, like Port-Royal before it.

The Eastern Indians, including the Penobscot and Maliseet, came into an accommodation with the British Crown in 1713. When they heard of the Peace of Utrecht and New England's efforts to induce the Abenaki into a peace, they were inclined to send delegates to a treaty conference being held at Portsmouth, New Hampshire. They were invited to attend the conference by way of the English at Casco Bay (near present-day Portland, Maine). At least three of the delegates who went to the gathering were Maliseet (by the names of Joseph, Eneas, and Pierre). The First Nations negotiators affixed their clan signs or totems to a treaty acknowledging that they were subjects of the British Crown and that the English might keep all their former settlements in New England undisturbed by the tribes. The English, in turn, promised the First Nations protection for "their own grounds" and free liberty to hunt, fish, and "fowl" (i.e., hunt birds). The Wabanaki also promised not to come into any future conspiracies to hurt the English.

A large gathering of the Wabanaki—men, women, and children, tribal elders and warriors—assembled at Casco Bay in mid-July to hear the treaty's provisions interpreted and explained. There were misgivings expressed and rumblings of discontent, all flowing from an abiding First Nations distrust of the English. The French exploited Wabanaki fears, intimating that the treaty's terms caused the First Nations to become slaves of the English.

The Portsmouth Treaty of July 1713 was put to the test almost immediately. The English not only reclaimed and reoccupied the ashes of their former settlements but pushed beyond those bounds. The First Nations complained, and tensions began to rise once more, encouraged by Father Sébastien Rale, the fighting French Jesuit who appealed to the religion and self-interest of the Wabanaki to resist any English encroachments. The priest had been the object of an English expedition to hunt him down in 1705 involving nearly three hundred English troops, but Father Rale gave them the slip although his mission on the Kennebec River was destroyed. Rale remained diplomatic with his English neighbors and quickly reestablished his mission following the peace but encouraged his Abenaki flock to be vigilant for any English transgressions.

Then there was the issue of the oath. After 1710, the Acadians resisted swearing an unconditional oath of allegiance to the British Crown for a number of reasons: religion, anti-British sentiments, fear of French or First Nations retaliation, and fear that they might be conscripted by the British to fight against those who shared their blood, religion, or loyalties (the French, First Nations, or other Acadians). At first, the British did not press the matter as they had little power to enforce their will in any case. British authority was said not to extend beyond a "cannon shott" from Fort Anne, but over time, as English power steadily grew, a desire to address the problem of the oath became apparent. The British resolved that they would make the Acadians into good subjects or force them to leave Nova Scotia. Many Acadians left the province of their own accord, seeking protection merely through distance from the English or under the guns of French forts in the region. Yet the Acadian lands from Annapolis to Chignecto were rich, and life was good. Many Acadians did not wish to relinquish family holdings that they had held for decades.

A showdown was inevitable. It may not come during the next war or even the one following, but it was coming. The British were intent on making Nova Scotia their own. The French, First Nations, and some Acadians were just as intent on reclaiming the whole of the colony for France by force of arms.

Battle lines were being drawn.

CHAPTER 4
Father Rale's War

Alas! What would become of your faith if I should abandon you? Your salvation is dearer to me than my life.

—Father Sébastien Rale to his Abenaki flock at the Norridgewock mission (Old Point, Maine)

August 1717. Paul Mascarene was pleased to be commissioned as a captain in the Fortieth Regiment, a newly formed British regiment raised in Nova Scotia and tasked with protecting its forts and settlements. The Fortieth was known as Philipps' Regiment after the governor of the day (Gen. Richard Philipps). It remained under the direct command of Nova Scotia's governors until the 1750s. The regiment was armed with a standard-issue flintlock with a range of two hundred yards, a short sword, and a bayonet. With their black felt three-cornered hats and red coats, waistcoats, and breeches, they resembled many British "line" infantry regiments of the day.

Born in Languedoc, France, in 1684, Mascarene was raised in Switzerland as a refugee of French Protestant (Huguenot) descent. Many Huguenot men who fled the fury of the Catholic monarchs of France during an age of religious persecution ended up joining foreign militaries fighting France in Europe and abroad. Such was the case with Mascarene who joined the British military and received training as an engineer. He was valued at his Canso and Annapolis postings as he spoke the language of the Acadians who lived in the surrounding communities and with whom the English of those forts hoped to establish closer ties. Many Mi'kmaq, Maliseet, and Passamaquoddy could speak French as well, and Mascarene was sometimes tasked to manage affairs with those tribes. It was no easy undertaking. The Mi'kmaq continued with their raids after the close of Queen Anne's War in an effort to keep the British from establishing settlements beyond Annapolis.

The British sought to win over the Maliseet by promising them "presents" (i.e., powder, shot, cloth, foodstuffs) and establishing a mutually beneficial trade. The Maliseet appeared uninterested in a trade at Annapolis but viewed the giving of "presents" as both an important economic and diplomatic gesture, normally binding them in friendship to the donor. The Maliseet were open to an award of "presents." The British thought that all the Wabanaki might eventually be reconciled to them in this way, just as they had to the French, but the French had always been careful not to settle any lands except with First Nations' consent, kept the tribes well supplied with goods, and furnished them with priests. The British, on the other hand, appeared determined to simply seize land whenever an opportunity presented itself, seemed unable to deliver on the promise of presents and hated the priests.

One such land seizure took place at Canso in 1720.

As the British started building a fort at Canso in August 1720 to protect their Nova Scotia fishery, more than fifty Mi'kmaq warriors and some French irregulars struck. The British saw three of their men killed and four wounded but took twenty prisoners, who were then sent back to Fort Anne. The British completed their Canso fort by the fall of the year (Fort William Augustus), staffed it with troops, and committed the Royal Navy to guard it.

Canso became a beacon for future Mi'kmaq raids.

Meanwhile, Father Sébastien Rale, who lived on the Kennebec River at a mission he first arrived at in 1698, was seen by New England as one of the primary instigators behind First Nations raids and resentment of the English. Rale, born in Pontarlier, France, in 1657, joined the "Society of Jesus" or Jesuits in 1675, becoming one of these renowned Catholic "foot soldiers of God." He volunteered for the American missions to the First Nations and was sent to work with the Abenaki of Saint Francis, near Québec, in 1689. After later service with the Illinois tribes of the

Great Lakes region, he took over the Abenaki mission at Norridgewock in Maine, where French clerics had been active since 1646.

From the pulpit at his mission church, Rale railed against the treaty of 1713 and condemned First Nations who might consider making any new accommodation with the English. He openly backed the demand of the Wabanaki Confederacy that the English must not settle east of the Kennebec River, being the old boundary of French Acadia. The English claimed that Rale went further, helping to arm the Abenaki and inciting them to acts of violence against the persons and property of settlers on the lower Kennebec. Rale pleaded tribal self-defense and protection of Abenaki land rights on behalf of that First Nation.

The First Nations claimed all the lands east of the Kennebec as their own by aboriginal right, but New England insisted that there were old, legitimate land grants from First Nations sachems to English Planters reaching as far as St. George's River (at present-day Thomaston, Maine). The Wabanaki disputed the validity of the grants. The English, in turn, sought to change the facts on the ground by converting an old trading post at St. George's (which the Wabanaki were pleased to accept) into a British fort (which they did not accept).

The completion of the St. George's fortifications in 1720—the same year the British built their new fort at Canso—made it seem to the eastern Wabanaki that an effort was afoot by the British to disregard their rights and hem them in from both the west and the east. Father Rale and the Wabanaki sachems complained. The mission at Norridgewock was reinforced by 250 Abenaki from Québec. New England, in turn, felt that it was on the verge of another French "proxy" war involving the Wabanaki. The tribes considered Rale at risk of capture or worse, but he refused to abandon his mission.

In an effort to silence Father Rale, the English sent a force to seize him in January 1722. Led by Col. Thomas Westbrook, three hundred militiamen converged on the Norridgewock mission but again failed to find the priest. They claimed to have found evidence of Father Rale's complicity in Abenaki raids. The English also hatched a plan to seize Joseph Saint-Castin, a surviving son of the "Old Baron," in November 1721. The plan succeeded. Under the guise of a friendly parley aboard an English vessel visiting Penobscot, this Franco-Wabanaki leader was kidnapped and imprisoned in Boston. He was kept a prisoner until the spring of 1722 when he was released in a vain attempt to demonstrate English goodwill toward the Wabanaki.

The Wabanaki were furious as a result of Westbrook's raid and the seizure of Saint-Castin. Although a low intensity guerrilla war was already being waged by the Abenaki in the west and the Mi'kmaq in the east, all the tribes in the Confederacy commenced hostilities against the English in the summer of 1722 after the First Nations Alliance held a War Council. The French were not involved, except as a source of material support: With no war in Europe, the French in America were careful not to start a worldwide conflict by openly backing the Wabanaki in their fight. French support and encouragement remained secret but substantial and was sometimes channeled through priests like Rale.

In July 1722, the Mi'kmaq moved to blockade Fort Anne in Nova Scotia, choke off its supplies, and force its surrender. They also seized and sailed nearly twenty English fishing and other vessels in Nova Scotian waters, retaining the crews as prisoners. The Maliseet joined the fight in response to the first attempt by the English to seize Father Rale. Royal governor Samuel Shute of Massachusetts and New Hampshire formally declared "war" on the Wabanaki on July 25, 1722.

The Abenaki of western Maine attacked the newly refurbished English fort at St. George's River. This palisaded fort, featuring two blockhouses, survived the assault. The fort would endure several more Abenaki raids as the conflict wore on.

A large Mi'kmaq-Maliseet force began to gather at Minas, Nova Scotia, for a final push against Annapolis. In desperation, the lieutenant governor at Annapolis John Doucett ordered more than twenty Mi'kmaq seized and held as hostages in order to prevent any major attack. The English also resolved to hit the Mi'kmaq hard and recover the more than eighty sailors being held prisoner with a raid on Jeddore, near Canso. At least seven captured English vessels were anchored there. In July 1722, after a two-hour naval battle that saw New Englanders, led by Ensign John Bradstreet, storm aboard their captured vessels in a hail of musket fire and hand grenades, the Mi'kmaq defenders were routed. In a scene reminiscent of Metacom's Rebellion, five Mi'kmaq corpses had their heads severed and placed on pikes around the English fort at Canso.

The British lost five men killed and several wounded during the fight at Jeddore. Nine English prisoners of the Mi'kmaq also died. The Mi'kmaq, in turn, lost thirty-five killed, many shot as they tried to swim from the battle. Other prisoner exchanges and tit-for-tat kidnappings continued elsewhere. At least sixteen captured English sailors were moved to the Mi'kmaq village at Richibucto, in present-day New Brunswick, for safekeeping.

Both the Mi'kmaq and Maliseet were active in Maine during 1722: The settlement at Georgetown on the Kennebec frontier was laid waste by a combined Abenaki and Mi'kmaq force, four hundred to five hundred strong, but its fort survived. John Gyles was in command of Fort George at present-day Brunswick, Maine, which he helped to build and then command beginning in 1715. He held the fort against the Wabanaki onslaught, but the nearby village was burned, and sixty prisoners were taken. Fort Richmond on the Kennebec River also survived a three-hour siege.

The Maliseet followed up on an earlier Abenaki raid by attacking the fort on St. George's River during a twelve-day siege in July 1722. Nearby buildings and a sloop (i.e., sailing vessel) were destroyed and livestock killed. Five New Englanders were slain, and seven more made prisoners during this raid, but it was claimed by the English that the Maliseet and Penobscot attackers lost twenty killed in a futile effort to take the fort.

New England was forced to suffer a repeat of the terrible Wabanaki raids of Queen Anne's War and King William's War before that. One can only imagine the settlers' terror at hearing an early morning Wabanaki war cry followed by the crack of muskets and warriors pouring out of the surrounding forest, determined to kill and capture. The smoke of burning timbers, the smell of gunpowder heavy in the air, the thud of hatchets, and the inevitable cries of the wounded and prisoners only added to this horror, but captives usually outnumbered the dead as they were valuable when ransomed through the French. The English of the frontier sometimes died by the hundreds if a major settlement were to be surprised, but routinely a handful of settlers would be killed or captured, here or there, if they lived too far from a local stockade. Needless to say, most settlements in southern Maine and New Hampshire lost citizens to marauding Wabanaki raiding parties.

English raids on Abenaki and Penobscot missions and encampments were no less horrific when the First Nations inhabitants could be discovered, but they often proved to be elusive. For instance, in March 1723, Colonel Westbrook led an assault up the Penobscot River but only found an abandoned Wabanaki fort, over twenty empty wigwams and a Catholic chapel, all of which he destroyed. Raids and counterraids continued into 1723 with the Wabanaki conducting more than a dozen attacks on the New England frontier during that year alone.

Acting governor William Dummer of Massachusetts ordered the evacuation of all the Maine coastal settlements into nearby fortifications in the spring of 1724 given the success of the Wabanaki raids.

Nova Scotia remained relatively quiet during 1723 except for a minor raid by the Mi'kmaq on Canso in July in which a handful of English were killed. In response, a new blockhouse bristling with cannons was built at the site. Meanwhile, Captain Mascarene was ordered to put the fortifications at Annapolis in a state of readiness in anticipation of more than just a passive blockade of Fort Anne by the First Nations. It was a wise move. The following year would see those preparations tested, but with the garrison of less than two hundred men and an uncertain ability to resupply the fort during a crisis, the future of Annapolis was at risk.

New England had resolved to strike back at the Wabanaki in 1724 in an effort to end their raids. The year did not start well for the English. In April of that year, a seventeen-man force under the command of a Captain Winslow was ambushed and nearly wiped out by hundreds of Abenaki on the St. George's River, south of the British fort. Misjudging the mixed motives behind First Nations hatred of the English, the New Englanders focused once again on the elimination of Father Rale. In August 1724, two hundred rangers managed to surprise Rale at his mission at Norridgewock. This time the priest was at home. He was killed along with thirty defenders, women and children. Scalps were taken, including that belonging to the priest, and these trophies of the raid were paraded through the streets of Boston. Abenaki survivors fled north to Québec.

The death of Father Rale

Pleased with the results of the raid, New England encouraged more scalp gathering parties to take to the forests. Massachusetts offered a lucrative bounty for First Nations "hair." Scalp bounties had been in place during previous colonial wars, but the price rose during Father Rale's War to between 100 and 150 pounds per scalp. Captain-elect John Lovewell from one of a collection of civilian bounty hunter units was initially very successful at this bloody work until an Abenaki ambush fatally ended his career in 1725.

In July 1724, the fears of the garrison at Annapolis were realized when sixty Mi'kmaq and Maliseet warriors surrounded Fort Anne, driving back a British force sent out to confront them. Two British soldiers were killed and scalped on the spot, a number wounded, and several outbuildings were burned as the siege began. The French later claimed that the British at Annapolis sustained ten killed and an equal number wounded during the course of the siege. A Mi'kmaq hostage was summarily executed by the British in retaliation for the raid, with the threat of more to come, but with no French troops or cannons to assist them, the First Nations warriors eventually melted away. The British burned several Acadian dwellings as a form of punishment for the raid and the lack of warning the Fort Anne garrison received from local inhabitants about the attack.

Canso was struck for one last time in the conflict when sixty Abenaki and Mi'kmaq descended on the place in the summer of 1725, causing half a dozen deaths.

The time had arrived to make peace. The Mi'kmaq had gained little, apart from maintaining the status quo by not coming into an accommodation with the British. The Maliseet seemed ready to restore the treaty of 1713 if a more stable peace could be secured. Just as New England thought that the way to stop First Nations raids militarily was to kill the French instigator, Father Rale, the English also concluded that the way to bring the First Nations into a peace diplomatically was through the French.

Exhausted by the frontier war, Massachusetts sent three peace emissaries to the governor-general of New France, Pierre de Rigaud, Marquis de Vaudreuil, at Québec in April 1725. The peace mission failed, but it set in motion a chain of events that would yield a peace treaty.

The Penobscot Nation was approached by the English about coming into a peace after the failure of the Québec mission. They responded that not only their own tribe but the Maliseet and Mi'kmaq as well were ready to negotiate. After some preliminaries, the main treaty was set for Boston in December 1725. The Penobscot alone sent delegates (by the names of Loron, Arexus, Francois Xavier, and Maganumba), but they declared that they represented the other Eastern Wabanaki tribes. Paul Mascarene had been sent to Boston by the Governing Council in Nova Scotia to protect that colony's interests. A satisfactory treaty was arranged which directed that further treaty articles must also be signed in Nova Scotia. John Gyles, the former Maliseet captive, served as an interpreter during the treaty negotiations in Boston.

Depiction of Wabanaki leaders signing the treaties of 1725–1727

It proved to be a long process. In response to a letter circulated by the council at Annapolis to the Wabanaki, the Mi'kmaq of Cape Sable came to Fort Anne in May 1726. They ratified the articles negotiated with Mascarene at Boston, and then it was the turn of the Mi'kmaq of the Annapolis River to come in. They arrived on June 4 and ratified the same articles. This was followed by a flood of First Nations: Penobscot, Maliseet, Passamaquoddy, Richibucto Mi'kmaq, Cape Breton Mi'kmaq, and on and on. The process did not end until the Maliseet of the upper St. John River Valley finally agreed to ratify the articles in May 1728. In the meantime, the British held two more treaty conferences at Casco Bay, Maine, in 1726 and 1727 in order to firm up support for the peace and ensure that all important First Nations parties were covered and cooperating.

At Boston in 1725, Paul Mascarene had made certain that the articles he negotiated would keep the Wabanaki from disturbing English settlements and assisting British military deserters. He insisted that the First Nations should submit their grievances to the British for redress and that all prisoners in the hands of the tribes be released. The Wabanaki, in turn, were promised by Nova Scotia that they would not be molested in their "persons, hunting, fishing and planting grounds," that they would have protection for their religion and priests, that they would have equal benefit of English law when it came to their grievances, and that they would be rewarded for returning military deserters (an obvious problem brought about by the isolation and iron discipline at the two British forts). All First Nations hostages would be released.

At Annapolis in 1726, these same treaty articles were ratified by Lieutenant Governor Doucett and the visiting leadership of the Wabanaki Nations, including, ironically, "St. Castine" (probably Joseph).

Father Rale's War was at an end. The two sides had fought one another to a bloody draw. The treaty articles of 1725–1727 reflected this fact. Exhaustion had set in among the combatants, and an uneasy peace was created although it would last for nearly two decades. During that period, there were no major outbreaks of fighting, but the Mi'kmaq, in particular, continued to assert their indigenous rights in Nova Scotia by threatening any English traders (even coal miners) operating without their permission and capturing and looting a ship or two. The Maliseet focused their attention on the English approaching from the west, and they became involved in the controversy over the legitimacy of English land grants, especially those at St. George's River, Maine.

New England continued to hold periodic conferences with the Wabanaki in an effort to keep the peace alive, but land disputes persisted. A combination of English forts, settlements, and wartime raids had pushed the Wabanaki north and east, away from the lower Kennebec River. Father Rale and his mission were no more. The remnants of the Abenaki concentrated mainly at Saint Francis (now, Odanak, Québec) where they remained a potent threat. The new "flash point" on the Maine frontier was the St. George's River fort and settlement, located close to the Penobscot River and its First Nations villages. Nova Scotia's small British population had survived the Wabanaki uprising of 1722–1725, but the Mi'kmaq, Maliseet, and Passamaquoddy remained in a strong position to renew the conflict if need be.

The British were unable to advance their settlements in Nova Scotia in this uncertain atmosphere and received little support from London. Meanwhile, the Acadian population was growing and expanding with nearly 13,000 souls as midcentury approached. If a new colonial war were to break out, the British at Annapolis and Canso (their only two settlements) ran the risk of being overwhelmed.

The Acadians, represented by their deputies, expressed a position of future neutrality in any coming war but still refused to take an unqualified oath of allegiance to the British Crown. In this stance, they were actually supported by Paul Mascarene. After various absences and intrigues while in New England, he finally took charge of the administration at Annapolis in 1740. With no means to force an unconditional oath from the Acadians, Mascarene settled for their promises of neutrality for the time being.

The situation in Nova Scotia could not remain the same indefinitely.

France still coveted its old colony but was gradually losing control over Maine to the advancing English. This put Québec at risk. More Acadians were moving into French-controlled territories near mainland Nova Scotia (i.e., Cape Breton, Isle Saint-Jean, and at Chignecto, north of the Missaquash River). This put the British in Nova Scotia at risk.

Both sides saw the ongoing situation as untenable. Both sides hoped for some event that would give them the upper hand in the region. The same was true in Europe.

Many thought that a new war was needed to "clear the air."

Chapter 5

King George's War

[The] misfortune at Mines was one of those things to which we are liable in war.

—Lt. Gov. Paul Mascarene on the British defeat by the
French and First Nations at Grand-Pré, 1747

January 1747. In a freezing tent at a snowbound military camp near Beaubassin, Chignecto, Jean-Baptiste-Nicolas-Roch de Ramezay, a senior commander in the French military, pored over maps of possible routes to the Acadian farming community at Grand-Pré (near Minas or Les Mines, Nova Scotia). At his side were two of the most capable French officers in Acadia at the time: Capt. Louis de la Corne and Capt. Coulon de Villiers. Outside of the tent, milling about, were a mix of French regulars, militia, Maliseet, Mi'kmaq, and other Wabanaki warriors. Among them was Charles Deschamps de Boishébert, a skilled Marine officer who would play a significant role on the battlefields of Nova Scotia in the coming years. Boishébert had already distinguished himself during the spectacular French victory at Port-la-Joye near Hillsborough River in present-day Prince Edward Island (then the French colony of Isle Saint-Jean). It was Boishébert who found some two hundred British soldiers on the island while on a scout for de Ramezay in the summer of 1746. The English force was foraging for supplies. De Ramezay struck immediately, sending five hundred French and First Nations warriors led by Commander de Montesson to surprise the unsuspecting English. His plan worked. Nearly forty English were killed and a number captured in this July 1746 fight. The English were prevented from subduing the Acadians in the colony of Isle Saint-Jean and were forced to withdraw.

De Ramezay hoped to repeat his summertime success and catch the British at Grand-Pré similarly unprepared, this time in the dead of winter. His planning would ultimately result in an impressive achievement for French and First Nations arms in Nova Scotia during King George's War (1744–1748).

Boishébert, de Ramezay's scout, was born in 1727 in New France. He served in the Compagnies Franches de la Marine or Troupes de la Marine, the only regular troops serving in New France from 1685 to 1755. Mostly billeted among the populace in the larger communities, they were also garrison troops at remote forts and lived among the First Nations if required by the needs of a reconnaissance or guerrilla war. In their coats of gray and waistcoats, breeches, and stockings of blue, they were easily recognizable. They, like their British infantry adversaries, wore a three-corner black felt hat and carried a musket, sword, bayonet, and on occasions, a hatchet. They sometimes dressed in First Nations-style buckskin, leggings and moccasins while fighting in the hinterland. They utilized snowshoes in the winter.

In late January 1747, de Ramezay resolved to hurl nearly 250 Marines, French Canadian militia, Acadians, and First Nations warriors, led by de Villiers and de la Corne, against the overextended English troops residing at Grand-Pré. The unsuspecting troops were New Englanders consisting of nearly an entire regiment led at the time of the raid by Col. Arthur Noble. On snowshoes, hauling their supplies on sleds behind them, the raiders left Chignecto, crossed over the Cobequid mountain range and pushed through waist-deep snow, fording ice-filled rivers and streams along the way. A journey which might take two hours by automobile today took the French and First Nations force more than twenty days to complete. As the raiders passed by Acadian hamlets, they picked up more disaffected inhabitants as recruits. They were also joined by more Mi'kmaq. Soon their numbers swelled to a force comparable to that of the New Englanders—five hundred men.

The raiders were within striking distance of Grand-Pré by early February and set about resting and preparing. Precautions were taken so that any Acadians who knew of the French force's arrival, and did not favor it, could not warn the unsuspecting English. Guards were posted on the road leading to Grand-Pré. Friendly Acadian guides from Grand-Pré joined the raiders at Melanson Village in the Gaspereau Valley, pointing out the exact locations of the English troops. On the night of February 10, 1747, the French and First Nations force was ready to advance on their objective.

A blinding snowstorm emerged to assist the attackers although it hindered their movements. The New Englanders, stationed at Grand-Pré in hopes of dealing a surprise blow to any advancing French force, were billeted among the Acadians in a string of twenty-four wooden houses. They were the ones about to be surprised. Except for a few shivering sentries, the English were all asleep. De Villiers and de la Corne split their forces into smaller detachments, each assigned to a particular English billet.

As the wind lashed the snowdrifts and smoke curled up from Acadian chimneys into the black winter sky, the attackers moved in. The surprise was complete. Many English never made it out of their beds. Colonel Noble was killed outright, but de Villiers was badly wounded and Boishébert was wounded as well. The French and First Nations fought house to house, pushing the English back. The New Englanders eventually rallied, taking refuge in the only stone building at their disposal, but it was too late to reverse the debacle. Running low on ammunition, food, and water, they arranged a cease-fire in the morning, and the next day, the surrounded remnants capitulated on terms that would allow them to depart for Annapolis.

The battle at Grand-Pré, 1747

More than sixty New Englanders were dead, forty more made prisoner, and a further forty wounded. French and First Nations casualties were more modest (thirty plus). The English were forced to retreat in the deep snow, unassisted by snowshoes and leaving their wounded in the care of the French. Many more English died on the trek back to Fort Anne from frostbite and exposure—one account indicating upward of 150. Upon hearing of the destruction of the regiment, Paul Mascarene sent a party of rangers to Grand-Pré in March 1747 to engage the French and First Nations attackers, but they were gone, back to Chignecto.

A classic French and Wabanaki raid had once again dealt a powerful blow to the British from Fort Anne.

But King George's War had not begun so auspiciously for France.

The war was the offspring of the War of the Austrian Succession in Europe (1740–1748). France and Great Britain were not drawn into hostilities until March 1744. The French in America, hearing news of the war, were worried that their sparsely provisioned fortress at Louisbourg might be isolated by English action. They struck first. Canso was raided in May 1744 by Mi'kmaq warriors and French Marines. It was overwhelmed. The unprepared garrison surrendered and the settlement was totally destroyed. Canso would never regain its former strength or status. This initial success was followed up by the first of four failed attempts to seize the last British outpost in Nova Scotia, Fort Anne.

Acting governor Paul Mascarene, realizing that war had been declared, took steps to put Fort Anne in a state of readiness to repel an expected attack. Having eliminated the British presence at Canso, the French governor of Cape Breton, Jean-Baptiste-Louis Le Prévost Duquesnel, lacking troops of his own to spare, recommended that the French priest to the Shubenacadie Mi'kmaq Jean-Louis Le Loutre raise a force of his First Nations flock and Acadians to invest Annapolis. Le Loutre dutifully complied. More than three hundred Mi'kmaq, Maliseet, and some Acadians surrounded Fort Anne on July 12, 1744. Their four-day siege inflicted only minor casualties on the garrison, and the attackers were forced to withdraw when reinforcements sailed in from Boston.

Le Loutre retreated to Minas to await promised French aid. It came in early September, and a second, more substantial siege of Annapolis took place. Capt. Francois Dupont Duvivier, a French officer and hero of the destruction of Canso, led the second attempt to take Fort Anne with a force numbering six hundred to seven hundred French troops, Acadians, and First Nations warriors, primarily Mi'kmaq. Duvivier arrived before the town of Annapolis on September 6, 1744, and set about establishing his headquarters. The next day, he called on Mascarene to surrender, the English position being precarious. Mascarene, in turn, called on Duvivier to surrender as more British reinforcements were expected at any time. The resulting siege would be one of the most dangerous episodes British Annapolis would ever face.

The formal siege began on September 9 with the Mi'kmaq and French rushing the ramparts of the fort at night while making more selective attacks during the daylight hours. Casualties mounted on both sides. The British officers at the fort were more than concerned about a possible French success and then slaughter or captivity at the hands of the First Nations. They asked Mascarene to explore surrender possibilities, but Mascarene did what he could to avoid any serious talk of surrender with the French. On the French side, things were not going well either. The Mi'kmaq were not impressed with a French effort that lacked both heavy cannons and ships. They had suspended a two-decade-long peace with the British and for what? Some of them drifted away.

The respective commanders—Duvivier and Mascarene—scanned the horizon each day, hoping for the naval reinforcement that might bring them victory. It was the British who would celebrate. On September 26, a ship arrived at Annapolis carrying fifty of "Gorham's Rangers," a group of hardened New England officers and First Nations warriors led by John Gorham of a prominent Massachusetts military family. The rangers immediately set about terrorizing the besiegers, hitting the Mi'kmaq camp and then mutilating the dead. The Mi'kmaq departed the siege, and soon the French were gone as well.

Mascarene was impressed with the work of the rangers.

Paul Mascarene

All that the Mi'kmaq and Maliseet had earned in return for attacking the English was a declaration of war leveled against them by Massachusetts and a new "scalp bounty" placed on the heads of all their men, women, and nearly every child: Every male above twelve years of age, one hundred pounds per scalp; every female, fifty pounds per scalp.

The Acadians did not rise up in large numbers in support of Duvivier's effort, and their commitment to the French cause was soon questioned in the halls of power at Québec and Versailles.

Still, the French were not done with Annapolis. This solitary target was just too tempting. To knock Annapolis out of the war was, in effect, to restore French Acadia with one blow, but as is the case in any war, the enemy gets a vote. If the French were bent on seizing Annapolis, New England was just as determined to take Louisbourg, the strongest and most threatening French fortification in the east.

The English strategy unfolded with an attempt in early May 1745 to destroy Port-Toulouse, a strategic French settlement in Cape Breton near Canso and a place of importance to the Mi'kmaq people. The raid was part of what would ultimately prove to be a muscular attempt by New England to capture Louisbourg. The first attack on Port-Toulouse failed. It was repulsed by French Marines, Acadians, and the Mi'kmaq, but a second assault on May 10 succeeded in destroying everything standing in the settlement. Other, smaller Cape Breton settlements were also raided, and the siege of the Fortress of Louisbourg began on May 11, 1745.

New England had managed to muster a force of 4,000 men and 90 ships for the siege of the French fortress garrisoned by some 1,800 French troops. The English landed several kilometers from the town, virtually unopposed. The Louisbourg garrison was in a state of near mutiny over issues involving pay and overall conditions at the fortress.

The Mi'kmaq, with some Maliseet and Huron warriors, were on their way to assist the French at the fortress in over fifty canoes, accompanied by four French vessels. They were overtaken by first, one, then three English warships in June 1745, near Tatamagouche on the Northumberland Strait. A two-hour naval battle ensued, and a combination of English cannon and musket fire raked the exposed First Nations warriors, causing what was described as "considerable slaughter." The French and First Nations finally broke off the engagement and made for shore in order to fortify themselves, but the battle was over.

There would be no relief for Louisbourg. The fortress surrendered the day following the naval battle, June 28, 1745.

With Louisbourg's surrender, all that remained of the French military presence in the Maritimes was a few scattered posts in what is today New Brunswick and on Isle Saint-Jean. The Mi'kmaq and Maliseet remained reliable allies but must have been stunned by France's weakness. The fall of Louisbourg came on the heels of a third futile attempt to seize Fort Anne. For three weeks in May 1745, two hundred French troops and hundreds of Mi'kmaq and Maliseet warriors again laid siege to Fort Anne, but with no naval support or heavy guns, the effort once again dissolved into a predictable pattern of burning outbuildings and inflicting opportunistic casualties.

The siege ended when the French commander Paul Marin de la Malgue was ordered by his superiors to break off the engagement and help raise the siege of Louisbourg.

He failed spectacularly at the battle near Tatamagouche.

During the May 1745 siege of Annapolis, First Nations warriors managed to capture one William Pote, a sea captain and merchant supplying Annapolis. In addition, nine of Gorham's Rangers were surprised by a Wabanaki war party while at their base on Goat Island near Annapolis and were seized. Like many captives before him, Pote's ultimate destination would be Québec. He was taken there by way of Cobequid (near present-day Truro, Nova Scotia), Tatamagouche, a new Maliseet stronghold at Aukpaque (near present-day Fredericton, New Brunswick) and on to Meductic. He and a ranger were both tortured by the Maliseet and Mi'kmaq at Aukpaque in July 1745 in retaliation for the indignities visited on the Mi'kmaq dead at Annapolis in 1744. After the long journey to Québec, he was eventually released in 1747. While imprisoned, he, like John Gyles before him, wrote an important narrative of his captivity.

With the severe blow to French fortunes at Louisbourg, France needed a victory to keep the Acadians loyal and the First Nations tied to their interest. They supported the Mi'kmaq and Maliseet in a new round of raids into Maine from St. George's River to Casco Bay during 1745-1747 totaling over twenty bloody incursions. The fort at St. George's River was struck three times by Mi'kmaq, Maliseet, and Abenaki warriors, killing more than a company of English militia and a number of settlers. While the Penobscot tried to avoid the hostilities, they were eventually drawn into the fire. Massachusetts responded to the Wabanaki raids with a new round of fort construction in southern Maine, including the building of a new fort at Pemaquid (Fort Frederick), but for the Eastern Wabanaki, the major effort would be against Annapolis in 1746. No one could blame them or the French for a lack of trying.

Led by a French admiral, the Duc d'Anville, more than 11,000 men in 64 ships were tasked with not only capturing Annapolis in concert with a land-based force out of Québec, commanded by de Ramezay, but burning Boston to the ground and raiding the entire east coast of the English colonies.

After the fleet departed France in late June 1746, a storm broke out near the French coast ravaging the fleet, which was then beset by disease. Off Nova Scotia, a second gale forced several vessels to return to France. Putting in at Chebucto harbor in late September, the fleet sat immobile for weeks while disease raced through the ranks. Meanwhile, de Ramezay's force of some seven hundred troops was actually doing quite well, reaching Chignecto in July 1746. Nearly six hundred Wabanaki warriors joined him there, but de Ramezay was forced to wait for the floating firepower offered by the Duc d'Anville's fleet. De Ramezay spent his time defeating the English on Isle Saint-Jean, then marched to Minas, Nova Scotia, still awaiting a union.

De Ramezay and the Duc d'Anville would never meet as the latter died of a stroke shortly after reaching Chebucto. His replacement, Constantin-Louis d'Estourmel, elected to combine the healthy remnants of his force with de Ramezay's men, then promptly attempted suicide. The expedition's third commander, the Marquis de Jonquière, continued with plans to take Annapolis. De Ramezay advanced to the outskirts of Fort Anne in October 1746 and made camp, awaiting the guns of the French navy and reinforcements.

They never came.

Jonquière had a change of heart and sailed for France. De Ramezay was ordered to withdraw from Annapolis. In response to de Ramezay's departure from Fort Anne, New England's martial governor William Shirley sent Arthur Noble and his regiment, first to Annapolis and then on to Grand-Pré, to lie in wait over the winter of 1746 in hopes of surprising de Ramezay on any return visit to Annapolis with his forces in the spring.

As we have seen already, it was Noble who was surprised by de Ramezay at Grand-Pré in February 1747.

King George's War was a vicious, indecisive brawl, but a final, sad blow still awaited New England. When France and England agreed to a peace in the Treaty of Aix-la-Chapelle (1748) the "status quo" was again restored, with Cape Breton and, therefore, the Louisbourg fortress being returned to France. New Englanders were outraged, having sacrificed blood and significant treasure to oust the French from this gateway to Québec. Their resentment was so fierce that Great Britain saw the need to provide monetary compensation (180,000 pounds) to the most impacted colony, Massachusetts, but Great Britain also had plans to secure Nova Scotia once and for all, with the establishment of new forts and settlements at strategic places outside of Annapolis.

The Mi'kmaq and Maliseet were probably left bewildered by King George's War. The stalemate on the battlefield prompted them to look to renew the treaties of 1725–1726 with the British, but with the revelation of what the new British plan for Nova Scotia might entail, the Mi'kmaq, in particular, came to see that Great Britain intended to settle fully one-half or more of mainland Nova Scotia, south of Chignecto. This the Mi'kmaq Nation would not accept, and the tribe was again encouraged by French soldiers and priests to resist British encroachments.

The Mi'kmaq resistance took the form of Father Le Loutre's War (1749–1755).

The Acadians, meanwhile, felt caught in a vise. Most clung to their promise of neutrality and avoided any open collaboration with French forces, but others, encouraged by their priests, with a wary eye on the First Nations around them, or simply looking for adventure in the midst of their daily routines, took up the musket, scalping knife, and hatchet when France called. Acadian participation in the sieges of Annapolis and the raid on Grand-Pré, though not widespread, was nevertheless obvious to the British. They routinely threatened to remove all the Acadians from Nova Scotia. The French population of Isle Royale (Cape Breton) was removed to France after the fall of Louisbourg, and the British threatened to expel the Acadians of Isle Saint-Jean as well. There was precedent.

The Acadians would have to tread lightly to avoid a horrible fate at the hands of the British.

CHAPTER 6
Father Le Loutre's War

I have Instructions from His Majesty to maintain Amity & Friendship with the Indians & to grant to those in these Provinces all manner of Protection.

—Gov. Edward Cornwallis to Maliseet and Mi'kmaq delegates assembled on board the ship *Beaufort* in Halifax Harbour, 1749.

April 1750. Father Le Loutre was alarmed. A British force of four hundred men under the command of Maj. Charles Lawrence had appeared offshore in troop transports near the village of Beaubassin (close to present-day Amherst, Nova Scotia). While French troops were camped nearby on a ridge to the north called Beauséjour, only Le Loutre, Acadian militia, and Mi'kmaq warriors were on hand to directly oppose Lawrence.

The British approach represented both a danger and an opportunity. The danger was that the British might establish a fort at Beaubassin, gaining some control over its Acadian residents. The opportunity was that the removal of the Acadians of Beaubassin, across the nearby Missaguash River to territory firmly in French hands, might represent the realization of Le Loutre's dream of the birth of a New Acadia beyond England's reach. To prevent the British from occupying an existing base of supply and sustenance, Le Loutre ordered the town of Beaubassin burned. The arson forced the British to retire and required the Acadians to relocate under the protection of French troops on the ridge.

Le Loutre's two objectives were accomplished, at least temporarily but at the cost of Beaubassin once again being reduced to ashes.

And Lawrence would return. In September 1750, with seven hundred men, including rangers, under his command, he stormed ashore and advanced on the ruins of Beaubassin, opposed by Mi'kmaq warriors and

Acadians established behind improvised defenses. Twenty British troops were killed, but Lawrence's men drove Le Loutre's forces from their makeshift fortifications. Horatio Gates, later an American Revolutionary War general and victor over the British at the pivotal Battle of Saratoga, New York (1777), served with one of the attacking British regiments. Once again, the French, with troops at nearby Beauséjour, did not intervene. France and England had come into a peace in 1748, and open, notorious hostilities were not an option for either side.

Victory secured, the British built Fort Lawrence on the ruins of Beaubassin on a low rise just a few miles from Beauséjour, facing the French-occupied ridge. It was a palisaded fort, complete with large wooden barracks, two blockhouses, and various supporting outbuildings. A "cold war" of sorts developed between the French, camped on the ridge at Beauséjour, and the English at their fort. Despite the European peace, minor skirmishes mostly involving irregular forces were routine including the October 1750 killing of Capt. Edward Howe, a member of Nova Scotia's Governing Council. The captain was seemingly lured from Fort Lawrence with a flag of truce under the pretext of a prisoner exchange. Howe, who had friendly dealings with the First Nations, including a role in the Maliseet-Passamaquoddy ratification of the 1749 Halifax treaty at St. John River, was feared by the French because of his influence with the tribes. There were whispers that the Abbé Le Loutre or Mi'kmaq chief Jean-Baptiste Cope, or both, were complicit in the assassination, but there was no definitive proof. In addition, a party of sixty rangers was ambushed near Chignecto by a smaller force of Mi'kmaq who killed seven, including the ranger commander Francis Bartelo and took seven captive—who did not fare well. The French, now under de la Corne, and, later, Commander Claude-Antoine de Berman de la Martiniere, were reinforced. The Abbé Le Loutre, meanwhile, directed Wabanaki raids on the advancing English occupation of mainland Nova Scotia. English rangers continued to raid across the Missaguash River "dividing line" into French-controlled territory, striking Acadian settlements with some success.

It need not have been this way.

In 1749, Edward Cornwallis, a British colonel, was appointed governor of Nova Scotia. He was fresh from suppressing the rebellion of the Highland Scots in 1745. His efforts to pacify the Scottish "Jacobites" were marked by plunder, destruction of property, and wanton violence. His approach was rewarded with success. He was sent to Nova Scotia in the aftermath of King George's War with orders to establish a major counterweight to French Louisbourg and bring mainland Nova Scotia firmly within the British Crown's grasp.

Edward Cornwallis

Despite his own inclination to "root out" the Mi'kmaq Nation, his superiors in London urged a peaceful accommodation out of fear that the Crown's now-conciliatory policy toward First Nations in America might be ruined. Cornwallis obeyed his instructions. One of his first orders of business upon arriving at Chebucto harbor in 1749 (the site of the Duc d'Anville's disaster in 1746) was to renew the treaty of 1726 with assembled Maliseet, Passamaquoddy, and Mi'kmaq chiefs. Ominously, only the sakamaw of the Mi'kmaq at Chignecto appeared at this August peace conference and none others of that tribe, but the treaty was renewed and further ratified by the Maliseet and Passamaquoddy in September 1749 at a ceremony at St. John River. Things appeared to be off to a good start. Restraint on the part of all the interested parties might result in a peaceful accommodation.

In reality, Cornwallis was landing some 2,500 settlers in fifteen vessels with two regiments of protecting troops in order to build a new settlement (Halifax) without Mi'kmaq consent, at a place of significance to that First Nation. The Mi'kmaq were not pleased. They caucused at St. Peter's on Cape Breton Island and wrote to Cornwallis demanding that he remove his settlement. Of course, the governor had no authority or inclination to do so. Instead, he embarked on an ambitious strategic plan to build forts at key Acadian settlements or placed so as to hinder any movements by mixed French and First Nations raiding parties. Where before only Annapolis had represented the British presence in Nova Scotia now the fortifications and settlements came remarkably fast. Besides Halifax, there was Dartmouth on the opposite side of Chebucto harbor (1750), Fort Lawrence (1750), Fort Edward (1750), Fort Vieux Logis (1749), Fort Sackville (1749), and smaller blockhouse-style fortifications guarding new settlements at Lunenburg (1753) and Lawrencetown (1754).

The founding of Halifax, 1749

When Father Le Loutre arrived in Acadia in 1738 to minister to the Shubenacadie Mi'kmaq, he had free rein to organize raiding parties and move about the interior of mainland Nova Scotia at will. After being captured by the English while in transit to France during King George's War, he returned in 1749 to a "new" Nova Scotia where British forts and settlements were springing up like dandelions. Enraged, he was determined to solicit the Mi'kmaq to once again raid the English settlements until France was once more at war with Great Britain and new support could be found.

Abbé (or Father) Le Loutre was born in Morlaix, France, in 1709. He became a Catholic priest and entered the Seminary of Foreign Missions in 1737. He was sent by the Church to care for the Mi'kmaq of Nova Scotia, a British Province with a large and sometimes hostile Acadian and First Nations population. He was zealous in the cause of France and was prepared to support and direct the First Nations both religiously and militarily. Cornwallis called him a "good for nothing scoundrel" and offered a reward for his capture. Le Loutre worked closely with Acadian militia leader Joseph Broussard, also known as Beausoleil, who organized one of the first major strikes against the Cornwallis plan for Nova Scotia: a raid on Dartmouth in 1751.

The area that would become Dartmouth was protected by a ranger detachment and regulars of the Forty-fifth Regiment of Foot. A woodcutting party in the area had already been attacked in late September 1749 by a Mi'kmaq war party. Two of the English were scalped, and two more were fully decapitated. Rangers were dispatched and, in their fashion, proceeded to scalp and decapitate a party of Mi'kmaq that they came upon. Upon the initiation of hostilities, Cornwallis dispatched troops to destroy the mixed Acadian and Mi'kmaq village at Mirligueche (later, Lunenburg, Nova Scotia) in October 1749. Troops were landed from the sloop "Sphinx" and leveled the settlement.

Governor Cornwallis, who was no stranger to inflicting harsh measures on the Scots, took a "leaf" out of New England's book and, in October 1749, imposed a "scalp bounty" on the Mi'kmaq based on French rewards for English scalps. The bounty did not deter the Mi'kmaq, and they struck the Dartmouth area again in July 1750, killing seven workmen. The main body of more than two hundred Dartmouth settlers soon arrived aboard the ship *Alderney*. In September 1750, a small Mi'kmaq raid killed five, and a hunting party was ambushed by the Mi'kmaq in October. Two more minor raids occurred in early 1751.

Dartmouth was a dangerous place to live.

It became even more dangerous when Broussard led sixty Mi'kmaq against the new settlement in mid-May 1751. Like most Wabanaki raids, it was a dawn assault. The goal was to wipe the settlement from the map. It very nearly did. Thirty or more homes were burned and almost as many English killed. Prisoners were marched off into the depths of the Acadian forest. British attempts to hunt the raiders down proved futile although a handful of Mi'kmaq were killed. A stockade was erected around the ruined town.

Dartmouth would be revisited by the French and Mi'kmaq many times in the coming years, but the 1751 raid represented an early test of the resilience of the British settlement effort. The British did not panic and passed the test. Dartmouth survived but just barely.

British forts were also the objects of Wabanaki raids. Despite their appearance at peace talks in the summer of 1749, the Maliseet, Mi'kmaq, and even Penobscot, along with some Acadians, struck at Fort Vieux Logis at Grand-Pré in November 1749. This former Annapolis blockhouse was moved to Grand-Pré in 1749 and transformed into a badly situated fort. When the attack came, sentries were killed and around twenty English captured, including six women. Attempts to storm the fort failed, however, and with the appearance of Gorham's Rangers, the raiding party disappeared toward Chignecto.

The rangers were put to work patrolling the road from Halifax to Grand-Pré, a distance of more than eighty kilometers, or almost fifty miles. While guarding that route in March 1750, they ran across a party of Mi'kmaq at St. Croix River, Nova Scotia, and a three-day fight ensued. Some abandoned Acadian houses and a sawmill were nearby. The rangers were forced to seek refuge in the buildings and send for reinforcements. Several were wounded. Cornwallis ordered regulars from the Fortieth Regiment with field guns to assist. With the arrival of reinforcements, the tide of the battle turned, and the Mi'kmaq withdrew.

The rangers proceeded on their way and later began construction of Fort Edward at Pisiquit, near present-day Windsor, Nova Scotia.

Robert Rogers, ranger leader, eighteenth century

Mi'kmaq raids across Nova Scotia continued uninterrupted, with only large parties of British troops able to move about the countryside with any assurance of security. "Pin-prick" raids were conducted by the Mi'kmaq in late 1750 and early 1751, testing the formidable Halifax defenses, resulting in a small number of British dead and prisoners. Halifax, a three-hundred-building settlement protected by multiple forts, blockhouses, batteries, redoubts, and enclosed by a palisade, could not be taken by the Mi'kmaq without substantial French assistance, yet the odd sentry, trader, or settler who was not cautious traveling on the outskirts of the town could easily end up dead or a prisoner of the Mi'kmaq. Prisoners, like those taken during the siege of the fort at Grand-Pré, the raid on Dartmouth or near Halifax, usually ended up in Québec and were held for ransom. Such was the case with John Hamilton, a well-connected British officer and illustrator, captured during the siege at Grand-Pré.

Even in the midst of the unending violence, the British hoped to entice the Wabanaki, especially the Mi'kmaq, to adhere to their treaty engagements. In the summer of 1751, Governor Cornwallis sent Paul Mascarene to attend a conference hosted by Massachusetts at the fort at St. George's River, Maine. Penobscot, Maliseet, and Passamaquoddy delegates were in attendance. Despite the absence of the Mi'kmaq, Mascarene held out an offer that if the Wabanaki would end their hostilities, come to Halifax, and promise peace, they would receive annual "presents" from the British, and a beneficial trade would be established.

The First Nation delegates promised to inform all the tribes of the offer, including the Mi'kmaq.

Edward Cornwallis never got to see the fruits of his diplomatic initiatives in Nova Scotia. Even though he repealed his "scalp bounty" in early 1752, his peace overtures did not appear to be paying off. Frustrated by the Mi'kmaq, colonial politics, and what he perceived to be a lack of support from London, he resigned as governor in October 1752 and left the province. He was replaced by Col. Peregrine Hopson, who had joined Cornwallis soon after the founding of Halifax. Born in 1685, this career military man had commanded troops at Louisbourg after its capture by the English until the return of that fortress to France in 1749. He knew the region and the Mi'kmaq. He proved to be more inclined to a peaceful resolution of disputes with the First Nations than his predecessor.

Hopson saw a glimmer of hope for peace when British offers finally paid dividends with the visit to Halifax of the Mi'kmaq sakamaw, Jean-Baptiste Cope, first in September 1752, then to conclude a treaty in October 1752. Cope's treaty renewed the 1726 treaty, "buried the hatchet" with the English, and saw the Mi'kmaq guaranteed "free liberty of hunting and Fishing," plus the other items held out by Mascarene in 1751.

Cope claimed to be acting for all the Mi'kmaq Nation, but in any case, events derailed the treaty soon after it was signed. A party of English killed and scalped two families of Mi'kmaq, claiming that they, the English, had been victims of a Mi'kmaq attack. Cope responded by rejecting his treaty—by some accounts throwing it into a campfire. The war was renewed.

An effort at peace also came from an unlikely source—Father Le Loutre. He proposed in a 1754 letter to the new governor of Nova Scotia, Charles Lawrence, that a cease-fire should be effected and an exclusive Mi'kmaq reserve of territory be established, embracing most of eastern mainland Nova Scotia, including the British fort at Chignecto (which would, no doubt, have to be abandoned). Surprisingly, the British at Halifax did not reject the proposal outright but were suspicious of it, thinking that Le Loutre was simply acting as an agent of France. The British resolved that if such a proposal were to be made, it should come from Mi'kmaq delegates. A similar proposal was presented to the Nova Scotia Council by a Mi'kmaq representative in early 1755, but again, the British insisted on a demonstration of broad First Nations support for the plan. The proposal was not advanced any further as a full-scale war erupted in the summer of 1755.

In August of 1752, the Mi'kmaq resorted to their old naval strategy of seizing English vessels, including two schooners and a score of prisoners near St. Peter's, Nova Scotia. In April 1753, Mi'kmaq chief Jean-Baptiste Cope (a party to the 1752 treaty) engaged in a sea battle near Jeddore, boarding and capturing a British schooner, killing all nine crew and passengers (except for an Acadian pilot) and then sinking the vessel. The Mi'kmaq continued to gather scalps outside of the ramparts of Fort Sackville in Bedford and the other Halifax area fortifications whenever the opportunity presented itself. Lawrencetown was beset by a large raiding party of Mi'kmaq and Acadians in May 1754, killing a handful of residents and soldiers and forcing the first temporary abandonment of the place by the British. Michael Franklin, a future lieutenant governor of Nova Scotia, was seized by Mi'kmaq raiders in 1754 and held for several months. He learned some of the tribe's language and cultural norms while in captivity. He was later made responsible for all First Nations affairs in the province during the American Revolution (1776–1783).

Le Loutre, who had helped to set all Nova Scotia ablaze, was increasingly nervous over the French position at Chignecto. The French land communications between the Fortress of Louisbourg and Québec seemed secure enough. The route ran from Cape Breton, along the Mi'kmaq-occupied northeastern shore of mainland Nova Scotia, to a new French supply post at Fort Gaspareaux (1751), near present-day Baie

Verte or Port Elgin, New Brunswick, through to Fort Menagoueche (1751), at present-day St. John Harbour, New Brunswick, and up the St. John River to Québec. The French added to that security by turning their military camp on the commanding ridge at Beauséjour into a regular star-shaped palisaded fort (Fort Beauséjour, near present-day Aulac, New Brunswick) and improving small fortified supply posts at Shediac in the east and Nerepis in the west.

Le Loutre added to the forces available to the French by encouraging the Wabanaki to collect at the Beauséjour site, but progress on the French fort was slow; a strong British presence was close, and Le Loutre did not help the security situation by siphoning off local Acadian laborers to build a cathedral just beyond the fort's ramparts. He also had them work on an irrigation project. A new commander at Beauséjour Louis Du Pont Duchambon de Vergor was not viewed by Le Loutre as especially competent. De Vergor seemed more interested in his own fortune than the fortunes of France in the region. Le Loutre would have been even more concerned had he known that a spy was providing detailed "inside" information to the English on French fortifications in the Maritimes, including Fort Beauséjour—Thomas Pichon, chief clerk at the French fort. Le Loutre would have been outright alarmed had he known that Fort Beauséjour was one of four sites within British-claimed areas that Great Britain and her colonies planned to wrestle from French control. At a high-level conference held in April 1755 at Alexandria, Virginia, among colonial governors and British commanders, including Maj. Gen. Edward Braddock, commander in chief of all British forces in America, it was resolved that the French Fort Duquesne in the west, Forts Niagara and Crown Point in the northwest and north, and finally, Fort Beauséjour in the east would be struck by massed colonial and regular regiments, almost simultaneously. Besides troops already in America, the British would send five thousand regulars to its colonies as reinforcements and could rely on a British American population twenty times larger than the population of New France to provide militia manpower for the coming fight.

A thunderclap was coming.

CHAPTER 7

The Seven Years' War

Come, each death—doing dog who dares venture his neck, Come, follow
the hero that goes to Québec.

—Lines from a song current with British troops
on the eve of the expedition to take Québec

September 1755. Charles Deschamps de Boishébert felt that it was time to show the British that there was still plenty of fight left in his French, Acadian, and First Nations forces. After several setbacks in the summer of 1755, including the loss of Fort Beauséjour, the French and First Nations resorted to a guerrilla war to prevent further gains by British troops.

The former British commander of Fort Lawrence, now present commander of Fort Cumberland (the renamed Fort Beauséjour), Lt. Col. Robert Monckton had already ousted Boishébert from a fort at the mouth of the St. John River, which the French had burned to ashes when retreating. Now he planned to send troops up the Petitcodiac River to destroy Acadian villages, round up the inhabitants, and expel them from Nova Scotia. Accordingly, he dispatched a sizable force of some two hundred New Englanders in two armed vessels to lay waste to Acadian holdings on both sides of the river. The force was led by Maj. Joseph Frye.

Frye and his force burned over two hundred buildings and left a detachment of about fifty men to put the torch to the chapel at Village-des-Blanchard, now present-day Hillsborough, New Brunswick.

Boishébert saw the divided British force as his opportunity. He led over three hundred French, Acadians, and Wabanaki warriors against the troops at the chapel. The smaller English force was hit hard with nearly half of their number quickly becoming casualties. In near panic, the New Englanders fortified themselves behind an Acadian dike and held off Boishébert's advancing forces. Frye returned in the armed vessels with the main force, providing some much-needed reinforcement, but after three hours of fighting, the British were forced to retreat and embark. French, Acadian, and First Nations losses were minor; the British reportedly lost twenty killed and six wounded. French sources later claimed English casualties in the neighborhood of forty killed and more than that number made prisoner. The defeat shook the British leadership at Fort Cumberland.

Boishébert's success resulted in the rescue of some thirty Acadian families whom he started moving north and east out of harm's way. Despite the victory, Boishébert must have known that time was not on his side. The British were growing stronger with each passing day and were striking everywhere. Twelve thousand Acadians were being deported. The French position was becoming increasingly desperate, with no reinforcements in sight.

Charles Deschamps de Boishebert

It had all started with the fall of Beauséjour.

Since King George's War, the French military had been content to congregate at Chignecto and launch or coordinate raiding parties into Maine and throughout mainland Nova Scotia. Now that state of affairs was shattered with the capture of Fort Beauséjour in June 1755. Beauséjour was the only British success of the "Grand Strategy" developed in the summer of 1755 of striking four French encroachments nearly simultaneously.

1. *Fort Duquesne.* The attack against this outpost at present-day Pittsburgh, Pennsylvania, USA, led by Gen. Edward Braddock, commander in chief, was an unmitigated disaster. Over five hundred British soldiers were killed, including their commander, and nearly as many wounded in a clash with a numerically inferior French and First Nations force. In a disorganized retreat, the British left the entire western frontier unprotected and open to First Nations raiders.
2. *Fort Niagara.* Massachusetts governor William Shirley's effort to take this northwestern French stronghold was bogged down in a logistical nightmare and never really get off the ground.
3. *Fort Saint-Frédéric at Crown Point.* Renowned ambassador to the First Nations allied to the British Sir William Johnson fought an inconclusive battle with the French at Lake George, New York, and could not advance on the fort.
4. *Fort Beauséjour.* The "cold war" being waged between Fort Lawrence and the French at Beauséjour turned "hot" in early June 1755 when two thousand troops brought from New England joined four hundred more regulars and militia at Fort Lawrence and struck out toward the French fort on the nearby ridge. The defending French could only rely on roughly five hundred regulars, militia, and First Nations warriors. In a flanking move, the British overwhelmed blocking French and First Nations defenders and occupied some high ground from which they could begin a formal siege of the fort. By mid-June, British artillery started to rain fire on the incomplete fortifications at Beauséjour. On June 16, 1755, one bomb in particular destroyed one of the

fort's reputed "bombproof" casemates, causing casualties. The French commander Louis Du Pont Duchambon de Vergor was rattled and immediately capitulated. Loss of life was small on both sides during the siege, but the consequential disruption of lives occasioned by Beauséjour's fall was considerable.

Fort Beausejour, 1755

Some Acadians were found under arms among the garrison that surrendered at Beauséjour. They claimed that they had acted under duress at the hands of the French and their Abbé Le Loutre, but Gov. Charles Lawrence of Nova Scotia had a reason—or some would say a pretext—to expel the entire Acadian population from the Maritimes. And he finally had the British and New England regiments in place to do the job.

Most Acadians had remained neutral in practice, if not in their hearts, following the fall of Annapolis to the English in 1710, but others had slipped away into the forest to join the First Nations and, occasionally, the French in raids on the British. They were rarely apprehended although the British had their suspicions. With Europe on the brink of war, First Nations raids in Nova Scotia continuing unabated, and both new and old British settlements in the province surrounded by Acadians, Governor Lawrence made his move. He ordered the expulsion of all Acadians from Nova Scotia when their deputies again refused to sanction the swearing of an unqualified oath of allegiance to the British Crown by the Acadian populace on July 3, 1755.

The refusal to swear such an oath was something the Acadians had done before without consequence, but now the British in Nova Scotia, encouraged by New England governors, had the means, motive, and opportunity to remove the French. British military might had grown steadily under Cornwallis and during the prelude to the Beauséjour campaign. There was no shortage of troops available for the Expulsion.

No instructions for Le Grand Derangement came from London. It was a colonial undertaking. The Acadians were clustered together in up to a dozen medium and small settlements, about 18,000 strong. Deportation orders went out from Halifax to British forts from Annapolis to Chignecto and beyond to gather together the local Acadian populations and ship them away in vessels to be made available for that purpose. They were disbursed mainly to Europe, the American colonies, the Caribbean and Louisiana (via France or overland from the Thirteen Colonies).

A depiction of the removal of the Acadians, 1755

In a cruel twist of fate, some British officers at Annapolis (and probably enlisted men as well) developed romantic, marriage, and family ties with Acadian women and were forced to deport those same women or their relatives. For instance, John Hanfield, commander of the Fortieth Regiment, married one Elizabeth Winnet, a woman of Acadian blood. In 1755, he found himself in a position where he had to deport his wife's sister, nieces, nephews, and other relations with no way, short of disobeying orders, of intervening. Ironically, the Mi'kmaq too saw many of their Acadian blood relations being deported by their British enemies with no way of effectively intervening.

The Expulsion was ordered while France and England were still, technically, at peace. The Seven Years' War in Europe (1756–1763) had not even begun.

Born in 1709 in Plymouth, England, Charles Lawrence, the man who oversaw the Expulsion of the Acadians, was, like Hopson before him, a career army officer who received praise from his superiors as a good administrator. He was also a fighter. He fought in Europe during King George's War where he was wounded. He later transferred to the Fortieth Regiment serving in Nova Scotia, where he was involved in seizing Chignecto from the French and building the fort that bore his name. As governor, he pursued a Cornwallis-style policy toward the First Nations, hunted the Mi'kmaq and Acadians with his rangers, and planned to introduce New England Planters to Nova Scotia to take up former Acadian lands. He was promoted to the rank of brigadier general in 1757 and participated in the siege of Louisbourg in 1758.

In Lawrence's talks with New England governors, particularly William Shirley of Massachusetts, there was an undercurrent of eliminating the Acadian population in Nova Scotia so as to replace them with "loyal" and land-hungry English and foreign Protestants. Yet the Expulsion of 1755 was also a war measure with a clear military objective: breaking the supply, trade, and military links between the Acadians and First Nations was a key strategic objective.

While many Acadians were caught unprepared and, initially, had no means to resist the Expulsion, the guerrilla war being waged by the First Nations soon exploded into a revitalized conflict, with escaped Acadians serving as new recruits. Chignecto was the epicenter of both British efforts aimed at expelling those Acadians who had escaped deportation and French efforts to strike the English when and where they least expected. In August and again in November 1755, the British raided the Acadian village at Memramcook, in present-day New Brunswick, arresting Acadians, burning homes, and killing livestock. They struck at nearby "Tintamare" (present-day Sackville, New Brunswick) and surrounding villages as well, accomplishing similar objectives, but as we have seen, when they attempted a raid at Village-des-Blanchard, Boishébert and his forces defeated them.

The British burn Acadian buildings at Grimross, St. John River, 1758

Immediately following the French surrender at Beauséjour, the small French garrison at Fort Gaspareaux, near present-day Port Elgin, New Brunswick, also surrendered. Soon this fort was the object of guerrilla-style raids. In June 1756, Boishébert sent a force to seize a British schooner lying in the waters of Baie Verte near the fort. Seven English were killed, a prisoner taken, and the vessel burned. Meanwhile Boishébert hovered nearby with upward of 120 men. After a British woodcutting party from the fort (renamed Fort Monckton) was ambushed by Mi'kmaq warriors in 1756 and nine men were killed and scalped, the British garrison of around 150 men abandoned and burned the post in the fall of that year in the face of ongoing threats.

Chignecto proved to be a particularly dangerous neighborhood for the British until 1760. While no major effort was made by French or First Nations forces to capture the new Fort Cumberland (Fort Lawrence too having been abandoned and burned in 1756), British troops who ventured outside of its ramparts were frequently ambushed and killed by the handfuls. Life at the fort proved to be tedious, but distractions like hunting or fishing could prove deadly for British practitioners if they were discovered by the Mi'kmaq or Acadian militia. In one instance in early 1759, a party of four soldiers and a ranger were surprised by the

Mi'kmaq near the fort, shot down, and scalped, with their bodies left to freeze into grotesque shapes in the snow before a relief party came upon them. As was the case at Fort Monckton, a schooner at rest near Fort Cumberland was attacked by Acadian and Mi'kmaq raiders in March 1758. They killed three of the crew. There is some evidence that a party of more than twenty rangers suffered a terrible fate while on a scout in July 1757 when they were wiped out, nearly to a man, in an ambush by Acadian and Mi'kmaq raiders. Only the ranger leader, a Lieutenant Dickson, and an Acadian guide serving with the English survived the initial assault, which reportedly occurred where the Aulac River meets the La Coup stream. The fate of the Acadian guide is unknown, but Dickson, who was wounded, was taken into captivity and housed at Trois-Rivières, Québec. He was only released following the fall of Québec to the British.

The rangers at the fort—usually a company known as "Danks's Rangers"—were a favorite target of the First Nations who both tortured and scalped members of the unit whenever possible. Of course, the rangers were renowned for visiting the same sort of treatment on First Nations, Acadians, or French captives. In July 1758, it was a party of rangers who ambushed fleeing Acadians near present-day Moncton, New Brunswick, capturing, killing, and scalping a number of them. Likewise, in February 1759, rangers turned the tables on Acadians who had ambushed them at Saint Anne's Point, at present-day Fredericton, New Brunswick, and not only killed and scalped some inhabitants, but are said to have tortured the family of the Acadian militia leader. British commanders did not think much of these actions. While they encouraged the killing of First Nations men and women, they tended to "draw the line" at the murder of Acadian or French prisoners. Still the rangers drew no serious rebuke from their superiors for their tactics.

Gorham's Rangers were probably the most famous of the ranger companies to serve in Nova Scotia. They started off as a unit of New England First Nations warriors officered by Anglo-Americans. Participation of First Nations warriors (Wampanoag, Nauset, Piqwacket, and others) remained a fundamental component of this ranger unit, but over time, the nature of the force changed with the addition of more and more non–First Nations frontiersmen. No "coon-skin" hats for these lads: they tended to wear either a jockey-style leather cap or a Scottish bonnet (one of the forerunners of the red, buff and green berets worn by the special forces of Western armies today). They wore coats of various colors, waistcoats, breeches, and sometimes leggings. A ranger company consisted of anywhere from 90–150 men armed with the standard-issue "Brown Bess" British musket, a bayonet, and hatchet. Casualty rates were high in ranger units as they were called upon to undertake many of the most hazardous missions, including battling the First Nations.

In May 1756, war was formally declared between France and Great Britain. Some historians maintain that this new war, the Seven Years' War, was simply a continuation of the last conflict, the War of the Austrian Succession. France and Great Britain seemed eager to settle old scores and Austria (France's ally) was determined to humble Prussia (England's ally). Complex alliances propelled the Great Powers into a conflict that would be fought around the globe.

In North America, the French won a series of stunning victories: the seizure of Fort Oswego, New York (1756), the capture of Fort William Henry, New York (1757), and the successful defense of Fort Carillon on the shores of Lake Champlain (1758). First Nations raiders—Abenaki, Huron, Ojibwa, Illinois, Shawnee—ravaged the frontier, but after staggering beyond Braddock's Defeat in 1755 and the French and First Nations victories that followed, the British started to slowly regain momentum, particularly in the areas where their fleet could operate nearby, as was the case in the Maritime region. They not only captured Fort Beauséjour in 1755 but removed thousands of Acadians from both mainland Nova Scotia and present-day New Brunswick, secured the lower St. John River Valley (where the British planted Fort Frederick at present-day Saint John, New Brunswick) in 1758, after capturing the greatest prize of all—the Fortress of Louisbourg on Cape Breton Island in July 1758.

With the capture of Louisbourg, the road was open to Québec, the capital of New France.

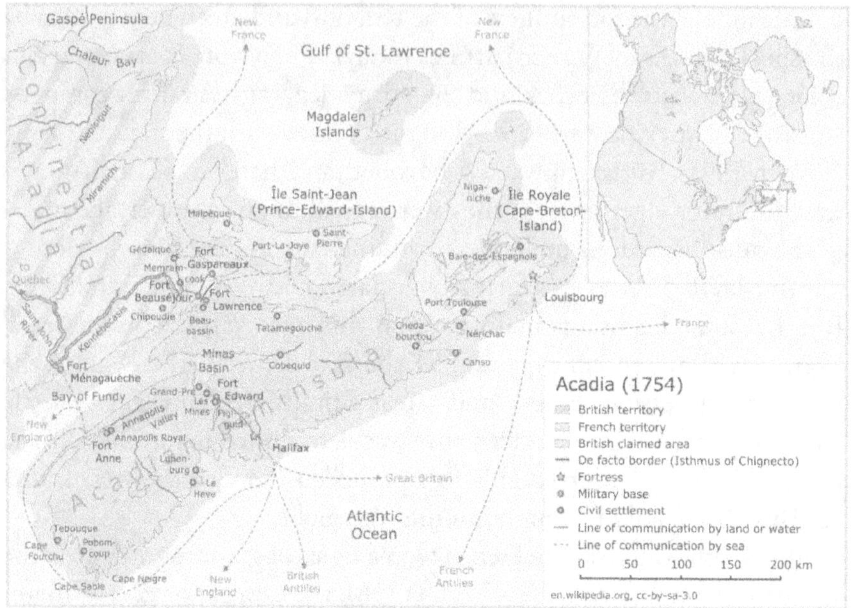

Acadia, circa 1754

Following the capture of Fort Beauséjour the remaining French, Acadians and First Nations did what they could to stem the advancing British tide. As "Britannia" ruled the waves, French reinforcement was not likely. In addition, the French Throne seemed more concerned about European conquests and protecting its Caribbean holdings than defense of its fur-trading empire in America. It neglected New France. The defenders of old Acadia had to "make do" with what they had against British forces that now numbered in the thousands. Still, in some places, they went on the offensive and had modest success.

Returning to a role they had played since King William's War, the Wabanaki raided the borders of New England, both immediately before and during the Seven Years' War. In the spring of 1755, homes were burned, settlers killed, and captives taken in the vicinity of Gorham, Frankfort, Sheepscot, and Gray in Maine and outside of British bastions like Fort Halifax and Fort Shirley, also on the Maine frontier. New Hampshire issued a "scalp bounty" applicable to the Wabanaki in July 1755 in anticipation of further incursions. Boishébert led Acadian and First Nations raiders against the fort at St. George's River, Maine, in August 1758, without success and also raided Meduncook, Maine, killing and wounding settlers, but the principal theater of war had shifted east.

Acadian and First Nations raiders attacked British vessels in the Bay of Fundy, and this led to British counterraids. Lt. Col. George Scott set a trap for Boishébert at Shediac, in present-day New Brunswick, in February 1758, but Boishébert ambushed Scott instead and killed two of his men. Danks's Rangers were sent out in June of that same year to clear the Petitcodiac River of Acadians once and for all. There was a return of Acadians to the area after 1755, and the rangers resolved to deal with the problem. Danks's Rangers, a company of "Rogers' Rangers" (famous for their exploits against the French on the borders of New York) and light infantry of the Thirty-fifth Regiment, burned buildings and supplies, took prisoners, and fought a series of running battles with Acadian militia led by Broussard into the late fall of 1758. Troops and the rangers continued to raid the Petitcodiac into 1759, driving the remaining Acadians to the edge of despair. Boishébert created a refuge for Acadian escapees, first at Cocagne, New Brunswick, and later at Miramichi, New Brunswick. Unable to keep the refugees sheltered and supplied with necessaries, many died or drifted away, only to be captured and expelled by the British.

With the fall of Louisbourg, the British also set out to purge the French colony of Isle Saint-Jean (present-day Prince Edward Island) of Acadians. The Acadians of the island had avoided deportation when Louisbourg fell the first time in 1745 and their brethren on Isle Royale were expelled by the English, but in 1758, the British of Nova Scotia were determined to eliminate any French, Mi'kmaq, or Acadian threat from Isle Saint-Jean. True, the island had served as a base for Mi'kmaq raids onto the mainland, but it was not a strategic threat. Yet a British force under Lt. Col. Andrew Rollo was ordered to take the island and deport all Acadians. A large party of regulars from three regiments plus rangers descended on Isle Saint-Jean. The French governor of the colony Villejouin surrendered quickly. The British built Fort Amherst at Port-la-Joye (near the site of a previous British defeat in 1746), and soon the deportations began. At one point, twelve transports filled with Acadians left the island only to have four of those vessels wrecked and more than one thousand Acadians lost. Some Acadians escaped the island with French help to go to refugee camps at Miramichi, Baie des Chaleur, and Restigouche.

Things were not that different on the St. John River. In September 1758, Col. Robert Monckton led a force of regulars and rangers numbering over one thousand men up the river from Fort Frederick, burning abandoned Acadian homes and barns at Grimross and Jemseg, New Brunswick. While the Maliseet may have had as many as five hundred warriors on the river, they decided not to tangle with Monckton's large marauding force. The remaining Acadians too retreated upriver.

Monckton retired to the mouth of the St. John River after advancing as far as present-day Maugerville, New Brunswick, and left for Halifax with the main body of troops before winter set in. A small residual force of mostly rangers stayed behind at Fort Frederick. In February 1759, in response to reports of a concentration of Acadians at Saint Anne's Point, at present-day Fredericton, New Brunswick, a party of rangers set out from Fort Frederick on snowshoes along the frozen St. John River in an effort to surprise the Acadian inhabitants. The rangers arrived at Saint Anne's and burned more than one hundred empty buildings, a chapel, barns, and storehouses, killing all the area's livestock. They were finishing their destructive work when they were ambushed by Acadian militia. The rangers won the fight and set about taking prisoners and scalping others. It was then that some members of the militia leader's family were reportedly tortured to death with beatings and hatchet blows in the presence of the captured militia leader, Joseph Godin, dit Bellefontaine.

After Monckton's main force withdrew to Halifax, the Maliseet invested the area around Fort Frederick, creating a situation much like that at Chignecto. British soldiers who ventured too far from the protective walls of Fort Frederick were sometimes killed or captured. In September 1759, a party of Acadian militia ambushed a detachment of rangers near present-day French Lake on the Oromocto River, killing nine and wounding three.

By late 1758 and early 1759, the French and Acadians had few sanctuaries left outside of Québec. Many escaped Acadians who could flee made the long trek north or west to that fortress city; others tried to survive hidden in the forest, at First Nations villages, or in remote hamlets. The British were meticulous in their efforts to gather up all the Acadians. Brig. Gen. James Wolfe led efforts to root out the Acadians from every bay, cove, and creek along the east coast of present-day New Brunswick and into the Gaspé Peninsula of the present-day province of Québec. Homes and fishing vessels were burned and prisoners taken. Wolfe detested the work. He wrote to Maj. Gen. Jeffrey Amherst, his superior, in late 1758, "We have done a great deal of mischief and spread the terror of his Majesty's arms through the Gulf, but have added nothing to the reputation of them."

In September of 1758, Wolfe tasked Col. James Murray with destroying the Acadian settlements at Miramichi in present-day New Brunswick. A stone church at an Acadian and Mi'kmaq gathering place was among the buildings destroyed by the British, leaving the site to be forever named Burnt Church. Boishébert's refugee camp, located farther up the river, survived the British raid when Murray's boats proved to be too large to navigate the waterway and his force withdrew.

James Wolfe, born in 1727 at Westerham in Kent, Southern England, was a brilliant and, by all accounts, brave soldier of notoriously bad health. Like many of his contemporaries, Wolfe fought in Flanders and Scotland during King George's War, replacing Edward Cornwallis at war's end for Scottish garrison duty. When the Seven Years' War erupted, he participated in the failed British effort to seize Rochefort, France. It taught him valuable lessons about amphibious warfare and the need to act boldly during such operations. His performance caught the eye of William Pitt, British prime minister, who sent him to America. In January 1758, he was appointed a brigadier general and joined Jeffrey Amherst for the assault on Louisbourg, along with Brigadiers Charles Lawrence and Edward Whitmore.

James Wolfe

Although France was clearly on the defensive during this new war in America, her militias and First Nations allies still took the fight to the British in mainland Nova Scotia despite the much more powerful British military presence now in place. In a last blow to the garrison at Fort Anne, on December 6, 1757, a mixed Acadian and Mi'kmaq force ambushed a British woodcutting party near the spot where the 1711 "Bloody Creek" ambush had occurred. One "grenadier" (a special assault soldier) of the Forty-third Regiment was killed and nine others taken prisoner, including six rangers. A rescue party of 130 men fared no better: On December 8, 1757, they too were ambushed not far from the "Bloody Creek" site while trying to ford the Renne Foret River. In a sharp fight with nearly sixty Acadians and Mi'kmaq, they suffered more than twenty killed but were able to break out of the trap and retreat to the fort at Annapolis. The French raiders suffered seven killed and nine wounded.

"Bloody Creek" had certainly earned its nickname.

Like the garrisons at Chignecto and St. John River, the troops at Fort Anne sustained occasional casualties and lost men taken captive as a result of Acadian and Mi'kmaq raiders hovering nearby. Fort Edward at Pisiquit was also the target of Acadian and Mi'kmaq raiders. In September 1756 and again in April 1757, British soldiers were killed near the fort; on the second occasion, some thirteen were killed at a nearby warehouse. The raiders helped themselves to the spoils from the warehouse and burned it.

The new settlement of Lunenburg was the object of nine separate raids over the course of three years, beginning with an attack by Boishébert and company in May 1756. Relying on Maliseet warriors living close to his St. John River headquarters at Saint Anne's Point, Boishébert led his raiders down to the south shore Nova Scotia town, wreaking havoc on its outskirts. Twenty or more settlers of all ages and genders were killed and a number taken captive, including one John Payzant. He, his mother, and sister were all taken in the raid. After four years of captivity, he and his mother returned to southern Nova Scotia, but his sister remained with her First Nations captors.

In response to the raid, Gov. Charles Lawrence revived the "scalp bounty" on Mi'kmaq and Maliseet men in May 1756, along with a reward for prisoners: Thirty pounds for a male prisoner above the age of sixteen and twenty-five pounds for a male scalp or the capture of a woman or child. He also undertook a raid on Cape Sable (a suspected point of origin for Acadian and First Nations attacks) where more than seventy Acadians were captured. A second raid by Maj. Henry Fletcher in the summer of 1758 netted a further one hundred Acadians. In an operation that would have been familiar to American troops fighting in the jungles of Vietnam in the late 1960s, Fletcher's troops cordoned off a large area at Cape Sable and then "swept" the place for inhabitants and any guerilla fighters. Captured Acadians were removed to George's Island in Halifax Harbour to await deportation. Lawrence also undertook the building of protective blockhouses near the endangered community of Lunenburg and staffed them with troops. The Lunenburg raids continued, however, and another thirty or more settlers were killed or captured. In fact, the raids around Lunenburg continued right up to the spring of 1759 and included attacks by both land and sea.

Lawrencetown settlement suffered a similar fate, and as was the case during Father Le Loutre's War, the settlers had to be withdrawn, unable to even leave their houses out of fear of attack.

Dartmouth, the site of so many Acadian-First Nations raids, was reduced to a population of less than eighty settlers by war's end (having been first settled with nearly two hundred immigrants). Even as late as July 1759, five settlers were killed in a raid on that place.

Scalps and prisoners were also gathered around the Halifax fortifications in 1757, with two Englishmen losing their "hair" at the foot of what is now Citadel Hill during the last of three raids in that year by Acadians and Mi'kmaq warriors. French authorities eagerly paid for such scalps.

Yet, with thousands of British regulars and New England troops, plus rangers, reinforcing garrisons in Nova Scotia and France providing no new troops and few supplies to that theater of war, the various French, Acadian, and First Nations raids, while disconcerting, were not decisive. Such was the case when the British moved to attack the Fortress of Louisbourg in June 1758. Led by Maj. Gen. Jeffrey Amherst, almost 14,000 soldiers, mostly regulars, in over 100 transports and guarded by nearly 50 "men of war" (sailing vessels armed with heavy cannons) assembled at Halifax in the spring of 1758. They appeared off Louisbourg's rocky shores in early June. The place was defended by around 7,000 French troops. The "Artois," "Bourgogne," and "Cambis" Regiments were present along with Swiss mercenaries.

The assault on Louisbourg featured a virtual Who's Who of the British North American military establishment including general officers Amherst, Wolfe, and the future commander of all British forces during the American Revolution—and frequent victor over Gen. George Washington—William Howe. Howe managed a regiment during the siege as a lieutenant colonel. Offshore, James Cook, later renowned as a Pacific explorer, served as master of the ship *Pembroke* in England's blockading fleet.

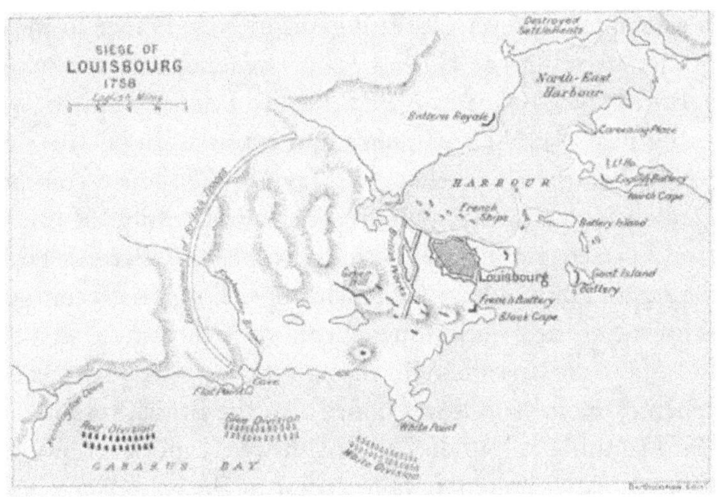

Map showing the siege of Louisbourg, 1758

A British attack was launched on June 8. Brig. Gen. James Wolfe led an amphibious assault, under fire, in order to gain a foothold. The attack ultimately proved successful, but an intervention by French troops, Acadian militia, and Mi'kmaq warriors very nearly stopped the assault in its tracks. A company of Rogers' Rangers bore the brunt of nearly one hundred casualties before Wolfe could support them with more troops. Once the British were fully ashore, however, the Acadian and Mi'kmaq contribution was reduced to skirmishing.

By June 19, British artillery was in a position to pulverize the French fortress. French ships in the harbor at Louisbourg were destroyed or captured and the town set ablaze. A French capitulation followed on July 26, 1758.

Although it was too late in the year to launch an attack on Québec, Louisbourg would serve as the staging area for the British effort in 1759. James Wolfe would lead the expedition. Jeffrey Amherst would be tasked with seizing Montréal, the "second city" of New France.

As Québec was threatened following the capitulation of Louisbourg, the forces of the French and First Nations again shifted their military efforts to the protection of that capital of New France. All the First Nations tied to France, including the Wabanaki, contributed to guarding the "Rock of Québec." Farther east, the Mi'kmaq made one final contribution to France within their homeland: When a French flotilla attempted to reverse British gains in New France in the spring of 1760, its arrival in the Gulf of Saint Lawrence was met with news that a British naval squadron had already beaten them to Québec. Anchoring near the Mi'kmaq encampment at Listuguj (Restigouche River, New Brunswick/Québec) on May 18, the French commanders pondered their next move, but the British were aware of the French squadron's presence and moved to intercept it. A fleet sailed out of Louisbourg and blockaded the French ships. The French commanders scuttled some of their ships, moving cannons ashore to form a battery. Nearly 1,500 Acadians and Mi'kmaq warriors provided protection for the French cannons, and it was hoped that the British vessels could be lured into running aground. The British were cautious, however, and moved in just close enough to shore to destroy the battery and hundreds of Acadian dwellings.

French vessels and their remaining cannons on shore continued to play a "cat and mouse" game with the British fleet, moving from place to place. Despite receiving heavy damage, the British ships destroyed all the new makeshift batteries. Any remaining French ships were then scuttled, but the British dared not send troops ashore in the face of so many Mi'kmaq and Acadians. The English sailed away to Louisbourg in mid-July 1760.

The fortress city of Québec came under siege by more than seven thousand British troops and a robust fleet by early July 1759. A bloody attempt by the British commander James Wolfe to attack the city from the east was repulsed. He then resorted to the tactics that he had employed against the Acadians of the Maritimes: he sent troops, including rangers, to destroy French settlements beyond Québec's daunting fortifications. Some 1,400 homes and outbuildings were destroyed, but the French, commanded by the able Louis-Joseph de Montcalm, would not be baited into leaving their sanctuary to do battle.

Wolfe needed a plan. He must come to blows with the French inside Québec's fortifications before possible reinforcements arrived from France or the winter snow and ice froze his besieging forces into their camps. He resolved to undertake a bold move. He decided to conduct an amphibious landing close to Québec, just west of the town, cutting off its supply lines to French-held Montréal. At a small cove known as L'Anse-au-Foulon, at the bottom of a huge cliff, an advance party of troops would land, scale the cliff, overwhelm any guarding force and allow the main British army to follow and prepare for battle. On the night of September 12, 1759, approximately one hundred French militia were guarding the cliff-top approaches to Québec. Their commander was none other than Louis Du Pont Duchambon de Vergor, the former commander at Fort Beauséjour. His forces were overwhelmed when the British gained a foothold on the top of the cliff and brought up their main body of troops. De Vergor, who was wounded, had lost Beauséjour. Now he was on the verge of losing Québec.

Montcalm decided to meet Wolfe on the Plains of Abraham, just outside of Québec's walls, where three thousand British regulars were waiting. Montcalm had a large but inexperienced force available to him, but not all were at the site of the crisis. There were probably only two thousand French regulars, supplemented by militia, First Nations warriors, and over one hundred Acadian volunteers ready to move when Montcalm decided to strike. The open terrain of the battlefield favored the polished British regiments who concentrated on breaking the French lines with massed firepower in European fashion. The skirmishing by rangers, light infantry, First Nations warriors, and French Canadian militia on the fringes of the battlefield had little impact. The fire from the British regulars was decisive. The French line collapsed.

Both Wolfe and Montcalm died of wounds suffered on the field of battle. Robert Monckton was one of Wolfe's surviving brigadiers. He was wounded during the battle but eventually took command. Monckton, son of an aristocrat, enlisted in the army in 1741 and fought in Flanders. He sat in Parliament but then elected to rejoin the army, this time in America, and was put in command at Fort Lawrence. The knowledge he gained of the Chignecto forts led to his being appointed commander of the expedition to seize Beauséjour. His success there, his efforts to expel the Acadians, and his good management of the campaign on the St. John River led to his appointment as Wolfe's second-in-command at Québec in 1759.

It was left to Jean-Baptiste-Nicolas-Roch de Ramezay (architect of the French victory at Grand-Pré in 1747) to deal with the aftermath of the battle on the French side.

On September 18, 1759, Québec capitulated. Although the French made a valiant effort to retake Québec with seven thousand troops advancing from the west in the spring of 1760, the city's British defenders, though badly mauled, held on until a British naval squadron bearing promises of reinforcements arrived in May 1760. Montréal fell to attacking forces under Amherst on September 8, 1760.

France lost the Seven Years' War. She also lost nearly all her remaining North American possessions by virtue of the Treaty of Paris, 1763, including "Canada" and the remnants of Acadia that her troops once held.

By the summer of 1760, the battlefields of Nova Scotia had fallen silent.

The process of brokering a peace with the First Nations had already begun before the Battle of Restigouche was fought. French priests like Father Manach and Father Maillard, who had previously led Acadians and Wabanaki warriors into battle, now arranged for the First Nations to swear oaths of allegiance to the British Crown or, in the case of the Acadians, to surrender, be imprisoned, and possibly expelled. The news of the fall of Québec in late 1759 started the process of Maliseet, Passamaquoddy, and Mi'kmaq First Nations coming into the British forts at St. John River, Chignecto, and elsewhere, professing friendship.

A Passamaquoddy and a Maliseet, Michel Neptune and Ballomy Glode, asked the commander at Fort Frederick to convey them to Halifax as authorized delegates for their tribes in order to submit proposals to the Nova Scotia Council for a more permanent peace. On February 11, 1760, they arrived before the council and agreed to come to final terms on the basis of the treaty articles signed in 1725–1726. The British also resolved to establish a series of government-run "truckhouses" or trading posts to ensure that the trade with the First Nations was predictable, fair, and did not involve the French. Soon Mi'kmaq representatives were also coming into Halifax, seeking an accommodation. The British resolved to extend the same treaty terms to the Mi'kmaq. A series of individual treaties with various Mi'kmaq districts followed, then a more general gathering at Halifax in June 1761. At this gathering, the hatchets of the Mi'kmaq First Nation were ceremonially buried in the ground, coupled with the promise that these instruments of war would never again be used to strike at their new "Brothers," the English.

Even the Acadians were eventually forgiven by the British of Nova Scotia for their alleged and real actions before and after 1755. On July 11,

1764, an Order in Council was passed allowing the Acadians to return to Nova Scotia, provided they were prepared to take an unconditional oath of allegiance to the British Crown. Many did, but finding their old lands forfeited and themselves displaced by settlers from New England and Great Britain, the Acadian returnees were forced to carve out a new existence along more remote and rugged eastern shores and far up the St. John River.

Great Britain had finally won on the battlefields of Nova Scotia. It had taken more than a half century.

In 1760, no one could foresee the ultimate consequences of a British victory—not the parties who contributed to it and not the vanquished.

CHAPTER 8
Aftermath

It is important for us, my brothers, that we exterminate from our lands this nation which seeks to destroy us. You see as well as I that we can no longer supply our needs, as we have done from our brothers, the French . . . From all this you can see well that they are seeking our ruin.

—Pontiac, Ottawa war chief, inciting an uprising of First Nations against the British

April 1763. Ottawa war chief Obwandiyag or Pontiac convened a council of First Nations tribes, urging a surprise attack on Fort Detroit (near present-day Detroit, Michigan). This former French stronghold, like a whole series of French forts in the west, had been surrendered by its defenders and taken over by British troops. Pontiac hoped to enlist any First Nations so inclined—especially former French allies—to take up the hatchet and oust the British from all tribal lands. Hoping for a return of the French (and encouraged by some French inhabitants), Pontiac ignited a huge uprising of diverse tribes that saw eight British forts captured and hundreds of British troops and settlers killed, but key British strongholds that were under siege (including Detroit) were relieved, and a combination of military expeditions and diplomacy ended the war.

Pontiac was assassinated years later.

"Wampum belts" (i.e., belts made of shell beads, which when examined by a knowledgeable reader, told a story or contained a message) were sent by Pontiac throughout the north and east inviting disaffected tribes, as far afield as the Mi'kmaq, to join in the uprising against the British. Neither they, the Maliseet, nor the Passamaquoddy did so. Nervous British commanders in Nova Scotia sought more troops to protect their now undermanned forts and adopted a conciliatory approach toward the tribes in the province. They need not have worried. There was no realistic chance of France returning to help the First Nations as Pontiac wished. With no hope of French intervention, any chance of the uprising succeeding disappeared.

Pontiac in council, 1763

In Nova Scotia in the 1760s, the Mi'kmaq, Maliseet, and Passamaquoddy seemed fairly content with a mild British rule and the advantages of a regulated fur trade at designated government-run "truck houses" (i.e., trading posts) put into place in accordance with the treaties of 1760–1761. While that trade would later be replaced by an imperial system of licensed traders, those measures still seemed to work well for the tribes, now totally dependent on the British for necessaries.

The reliance on any sort of truck-house trade was discontinued in the Maritimes following the American Revolution. As the availability of fur-bearing animals proved problematic and markets disappeared, the Mi'kmaq, Maliseet, and Passamaquoddy diversified their economies and became lumberjacks, craftspeople, farm laborers, and guides for local, European, and American "sports" (sport hunters, fishers, etc.).

In later years, the Wabanaki would be overcome by scores of immigrants hungry for land and by indigence. Pushed by waves of advancing settlers into small reserved tracts, by the mid-1840s, the Mi'kmaq and Maliseet were so destitute that the Maritime provinces started to sell off the best remaining Indian Reserve lands to non-Indian settlers (mainly squatters) in hopes of creating funds to assist the tribes. Reduced to even smaller tracts of protected territory, it has only been since the Second World War that the First Nations have been able to break out of their stagnant circumstances and make major political, economic, educational, and cultural gains.

The Passamaquoddy Experience mirrored that of their Canadian neighbors: The Passamaquoddy had largely been relegated to the American side of the international frontier following the American Revolution. They too suffered poverty and neglect at the hands of the state of Maine and the United States but experienced a rebirth in the twentieth century. Apart from the Penobscot, who were neighbors to the Passamaquoddy, only a few remnants of the other Wabanaki Nations even survived the conflicts, which ended in 1760, yet so fierce was the Wabanaki resistance to British colonization in the northeast prior to 1760 that some researchers have speculated that this resistance and a lingering fear of the tribes among potential New England settlers pushed the tide of settlement and eventual urbanization and development, west instead of east.

The treaties renewed with the First Nations of Nova Scotia in 1760 and 1761 promised respect for aboriginal hunting grounds and access to natural resources but were imprecise beyond such broad guarantees. Any British plan to slowly address the First Nations land issue on a piecemeal basis was blasted first by the unexpected arrival of the United Empire Loyalist refugees from the American Revolution (1776–1783) and, later, by immigration from Europe. The great resource of "territory" was denied to the tribes.

In 1746, a New England trader and sometime lobbyist William Vaughan surmised that a final land settlement with the First Nations tribes of Nova Scotia could be procured with just a portion of a twenty-thousand-pound gratuity set aside by the British Crown for better securing that province.

Today, a land settlement with the Mi'kmaq, Maliseet, and Passamaquoddy peoples, premised on unextinguished aboriginal land title and treaty guarantees would probably cost Canada and the provinces involved multimillions of dollars along with land transfers and other accommodations.

The Acadians not only rebounded from their forced exile in 1755 but eventually thrived and extended their cultural and political influence throughout the Maritime region. Any hope by British commanders involved in the Expulsion of 1755 and resulting guerrilla war that the Acadians would be utterly destroyed as a people quickly proved to be a false hope, but for decades, the Acadians suffered from religious, social, and linguistic discrimination. The Acadians survived and evolved into a strong and vibrant element of our Maritime society: education, cooperation, and eventually, political engagement propelled Acadian society forward.

British plans to transform Nova Scotia and its other North American colonies into loyal recipients of its population, and products were soon derailed by the Thirteen American Colonies' rejection of those plans in the form of the American Revolution. While this rebellion resulted in a brief uprising by a mixed group of disillusioned First Nations leaders and discontented New England settlers in Nova Scotia, it was not a general revolt by any means, both the First Nations and the settler community sharing the problem of divided loyalties. Despite a direct plea by George Washington designed to entice the Wabanaki into joining America and striking "Old England," the majority of the First Nations held fast to their treaty relationship with the Crown, and most settlers too stayed loyal. The Acadians remained loyal to their oath of allegiance.

Only a few significant acts of violence occurred during the revolution within mainland Nova Scotia, the most dangerous episode being a failed siege of Fort Cumberland at Chignecto by revolutionaries and their First Nation allies in late 1776. Nova Scotia was also the victim of American "privateering" during the war with many Maritime ports being raided from the sea, pillaged and burned, but it seems that the province "gave" as good as it "got" in that department, fitting out and sending to sea numerous armed vessels for the purpose of raiding American commerce. Many an American "prize" was taken and the spoils divided between Crown and crew. This would be an activity that seafaring Maritimers would gainfully continue during the upcoming War of 1812 with the United States.

Conclusion

Any visitor to Nova Scotia, New Brunswick, or portions of the state of Maine looking for vast colonial war-era battlefields of the kind found in the United States at Yorktown (American Revolution), Gettysburg (American Civil War), or in Europe at Waterloo (Napoleonic Wars) might be disappointed. With the exceptions of Beauséjour or Louisbourg, extensive parklands are not dedicated to the French, British, and First Nations struggles that swept over the northeast from the 1670s until 1760, but that does not mean there are no "battlefields." There are patches of ground from Pemaquid to St. George's River in Maine through to Nashwaak and Hillsborough, New Brunswick, and on into the Annapolis Valley, round Cape Sable, and through to Lunenburg and Halifax, Nova Scotia, and beyond, where men fought desperate battles, grappling with one another using hatchets, knives, and muskets. No doubt, they hoped to survive the immediate fight, but they also hoped to achieve the greater objectives of their colonial masters or First Nations.

Today, some of these battlefields are marked with a worn stone cairn and a plaque; many, not at all. Yet these places deserve visitation or at least remembrance as testaments to the deceased men, women, and children associated with the sites. The French, British, and First Nations combatants or innocents who shed blood on those patches of ground believed as strongly in their dreams and aspirations as did any warriors or victims of war from our later conflicts: they all helped to shape our collective heritage.

"War" is sometimes defined as political violence. The violence can be conducted by nation states or by so-called "non-state" actors in order to achieve strongly held objectives. These objectives may range from enhancing an empire's "sphere of influence" to simply preserving a threatened society or way of life.

Did the principal actors who fought on the battlefields of Nova Scotia achieve their objectives?

If France fought to preserve and enlarge a North American empire, that objective was dashed on the cliff tops of Québec. Not until the rise of Napoleon would French imperial aspirations send her armies overseas once again, but not in an effort to retake "New France."

If the First Nations fought to preserve their independence, freedom of action, and unlimited control over their vast territories, it cannot be said that they achieved their objectives. Still, they have survived as distinct peoples against enormous odds, living within the same territories that their forefathers once fought to hold. The colonial wars brought death, disease, and disruption to First Nations societies, which led, in turn, to grinding poverty and colonial government paternalism. Today, many First Nations members reside within communities where they have only limited governance under a piece of alien legislation (the federal "Indian Act"), reduced to occupying small First Nation land "reserves."

If the Acadians fought in order to be left alone so that their farming communities and lifestyle immersed in the Catholic faith could survive, they too cannot be said to have achieved their objectives. Their townships were broken up, their families separated, expelled, and scattered. It has been a hard but amazing road leading to the rebirth of a robust Acadian society in our region. An especially strong revival has taken place, ironically, in the areas where Abbé Le Loutre sought to build his New Acadia away from British influences in mainland Nova Scotia.

If the British fought to achieve imperial objectives, plant their colonists throughout "old" Nova Scotia and smash the power of the French and First Nations forever, they were fairly successful, but their allies in New England quickly turned on them during the American Revolution and became both strong enemies and even stronger allies of Great Britain in later years. The Maritime provinces have narrowly escaped absorption into the United States on several occasions, mainly with the help of the Royal Navy. Economic prosperity has come and gone. What were once mainly European societies in the Maritimes have become multiethnic and multicultural.

After being dispossessed of their territories and seeing their treaties ignored for decades, the First Nations are now asserting a new confidence. They are fighting for their asserted rights in the halls of justice and corridors of power: these are the new "battlefields." Many First Nations members, in cooperation with non-First Nations peoples, are at the forefront of opposing large-scale resource development by private corporations on provincial lands. Is this any great surprise given the First Nations' history?

The resurgence of "Acadia" could never have been foreseen by even its most ardent, early supporters. Acadians are no longer a farm-based, Catholic-directed people although many Acadians are still farmers or Catholics or both. But the New Acadia is a thoroughly modern mixed faith community, strongly entrepreneurial, with a powerful political drive. What would Abbé Le Loutre think of this New Acadia?

In 2014, New Brunswick once again elected a premier and government leader of Acadian ancestry.

The British too emerged from a colonial past of autocratic, centralized governments in their provinces of Nova Scotia and, after separation in 1784, New Brunswick, through a combination of political reforms, Confederation in 1867 and transformation into governments and societies based on universal suffrage, constitutional freedoms, and democratic ideals. The British achieved these remarkable objectives over time, but clearly these were not objectives that they envisaged or even supported in 1755.

War is a strange undertaking; you do not always obtain from it what you initially want to achieve, even if you are mostly successful.

What happened to some of the key individual actors who appeared on the battlefields of Nova Scotia?

- Benjamin Church, the originator of the ranger companies, wrote about his wartime exploits and died at home in Rhode Island in 1718.
- Jean-Vincent d'Abbadie de Saint-Castin, French baron and convert to a First Nation's way of life, returned to France to defend his hereditary title and estates and eventually died there in 1707.

- Joseph Robineau de Villebon, governor of Acadia and defender of Fort Nashwaak, who was a son of New France, died in Acadia in 1700.
- Paul Mascarene, the Huguenot lieutenant governor of Nova Scotia and defender of Fort Anne on several occasions, died poor in Boston, Massachusetts, in 1760. He is best known for either personally negotiating or being involved in the negotiation of many of the treaties with the Wabanaki tribes including those of 1725, 1726, and 1749.
- Charles Deschamps de Boishébert, the French Marine and hero of the Acadian resistance to the Expulsion of 1755, participated in the defence of Québec, and remained interested and involved in the fate of the Acadians. He died in France in 1797.
- Edward Cornwallis, founder of Halifax and the architect of the final, successful strategy to win Nova Scotia for the British, fought the French in Europe (not without controversy), and died at Gibraltar where he was governor in 1776.
- Charles Lawrence, first commander of Fort Lawrence and, later, architect of the deportation of the Acadians while governor of Nova Scotia, died of pneumonia at Halifax in 1760, a place he helped to establish and defend.
- Robert Monckton, Wolfe's Second at Québec, went on to further acclaim, commanding the effort to capture Martinique and other French sugar islands in 1762, becoming governor of New York in 1763 and then holding several high administrative posts in Britain until his death in 1782.
- Jean-Baptiste-Nicolas-Roch de Ramezay left "Canada" after the fall of Québec, lived in France on a modest pension and died in 1777.
- Joseph Broussard, known as Beausoleil, Acadian rebel and guerrilla fighter during four of the six colonial wars in Nova Scotia, died in Louisiana around 1765 after finally being apprehended by the British, imprisoned, and then deported, first to Dominica in the Caribbean, and then making his way to Louisiana.
- Jeffrey Amherst, conqueror of both Louisbourg and Montréal, first British governor over the territories that had once comprised

New France, adversary of Pontiac and, later, a baron in Great Britain, died at his English estate Montréal Park in 1797.

— Abbé Le Loutre, spiritual and military leader among the Acadians and Mi'kmaq and architect of an insurgency waged against the British of Nova Scotia escaped the siege of Beauséjour only to be later captured and imprisoned by the British. He was released after the Peace of 1763 and died in France in 1772.

Other actors, such as Father Sabastien Rale, Mi'kmaq war chief sakamaw Jean-Baptiste Cope or the regimental commander at Grand-Pré in 1747 Arthur Noble died, or in Cope's case, probably died, on the battlefields of "old" Nova Scotia, along with hundreds of others.

If you walk upon the many colonial battlefields of "old" Nova Scotia and consider the people and places that strongly contributed to who and what we are today as a society, do not be surprised if your imagination takes you back to a time when the sounds of cannon fire filled the air, the crash of muskets was heard, and the war cry of the Wabanaki signaled that fierce combat was about to erupt in battleground Nova Scotia.

Notes

1. I refer to both "Maine" and "New Brunswick" throughout the text, but neither existed as its own autonomous jurisdiction during the period in which the events transpired as related in this book. "Maine" was simply a "district" claimed by both France and Massachusetts but, except at its southern limits, was largely peopled by First Nations. "New Brunswick," while not bearing that name, formed a portion of first, Acadia and later, Nova Scotia before being erected into a separate colony in 1784; therefore, when I refer to "Maine" or "New Brunswick" in the text, I am simply referring to the general geographic areas which, today, form separate American and Canadian jurisdictions.

2. I refer to the "Wabanaki" in this book, denoting a confederacy of eastern First Nations tribes that was certainly active before 1760. The Abenaki of western Maine were associated with the confederacy, but their grouping consisted of several small, distinct nations. The Mi'kmaq were members of this alliance, but their traditions, language, and customs were quite unique when compared with their Wabanaki neighbors. The Maliseet, Passamaquoddy, and Penobscot were all closely aligned politically, militarily, and culturally and spoke variations of the same language, an Algonquian dialect.

3. Dating the occurrence of some of the events in this text was difficult given that before September 2, 1752, the French and British calendars did not align. There is a difference of between ten or eleven days in the dates recorded by these European powers for significant events. I have chosen, for the most part, to cite the most commonly used dates for specific events (be they French or British), or I simply refer to the time of the month an event occurred.

4. I refer to both the "English" and the "British" interchangeably throughout the text, but as any Scot may tell you, to be "British" is not necessarily to be "English." The Scottish and English nations formed a political union in 1706–1707. Some ethnic Scots and the English continued to be at odds, culminating in a failed Scottish uprising in 1745. The use of the terms "English" and "British" interchangeably is mostly a convenience on my part and does not strictly denote eighteenth century political or ethnic realities.

5. Both the terms "sachem" and "sakamaw" are used in the text and roughly translate from First Nations dialects into an English description of a First Nations "chief" or headman, the former being a term commonly used for Abenaki and other Wabanaki leaders, exclusive of the Mi'kmaq, and the latter being the actual Mi'kmaq term of reference but sometimes used by the British.

Related Readings

1. Baxter, James Phinney, ed. *Documentary History of the State of Maine.* 24 vols. Maine Historical Society: Brown Thurston and Company, 1889.

2. Charlevoix, Pierre Francois-Xavier. History and General Description of New France. Translated by John Gilmary Shea. 3 vols. New York, 1866.

3. Dale, Ronald J. *The Fall of New France.* James Lorimer and Company Limited: Toronto, 2004.

4. Grenier, John. *The Far Reaches of Empire: War in Nova Scotia, 1710–1760.* University of Oklahoma Press: Norman, 2008.

5. W. D. Hamilton and W. A. Spray. *Source Materials Relating to the New Brunswick Indian.* Hamray Books: Fredericton, 1977.

6. Morrison, Kenneth M. *The Embattled Northeast.* University of California Press: Berkeley and Los Angeles, 1984.

7. Murdoch, Beamish. *A History of Nova Scotia, or Acadie.* 3 vols. John Burns, Printer and Publisher: Halifax, 1866.

8. Parkman, Francis. *Montcalm and Wolfe.* Collier Books: New York, 1969.

9. Wicken, William. *Mi'kmaq Treaties on Trial: History, Land, and Donald Marshall Junior.* University of Toronto Press, 2002.

About the Book

This is a story of a clash of cultures and battle for territorial supremacy. It took place in the 17th and 18th centuries in 'old' Nova Scotia. The Nova Scotia of today is an eastern Canadian Province, but 300 years ago name "Nova Scotia" was applied to an area stretching from what is, today, the State of Maine through the Province of New Brunswick and on into peninsular Nova Scotia. Even before that time, the same territory was known as the French colony of "Acadia". It was peopled by Aboriginal tribes, then the French and finally an English presence beginning in 1710. That presence sparked a conflict between the Aboriginal First Nations, allied with the French, and the British for control of 'old' Nova Scotia. While the three cultures clashed even before 1710, their warfare intensified after the British seized control of their new colony of Nova Scotia by capturing its capital, Annapolis. The French and First Nations violently contested British control over Nova Scotia through a series of raids, sieges, and pitched battles which only ended with a British victory in 1760.

This book identifies the events, people and places associated with nearly 85 years of struggle between the Aboriginal Peoples, the French and the British for possession of Battlefield Nova Scotia.

Index

bounties xv, 36
Bourgogne 76
Braddock, Edward 60, 63
Bradstreet, John 33
British ix, xi, xiii, xv, xvi, xvii, xviii, 5,
    6, 13, 25, 26, 27, 28, 29, 30, 31, 32,
    34, 35, 36, 37, 38, 39, 40, 41, 42,
    44, 45, 50, 51, 52, 53, 54, 55, 56,
    57, 58, 59, 60, 61, 62, 63, 64, 65, 66,
    67, 68, 69, 70, 71, 72, 73, 74, 75, 76,
    77, 78, 79, 80, 81, 82, 83, 84, 85, 87,
    88, 89, 90, 91, 93, 94, 97
Broussard, Joseph 55, 90
Brown Bess 69
Brunswick ix, x, xvi, 11, 18, 21, 27, 28,
    34, 47, 48, 60, 61, 66, 67, 68, 69, 71,
    72, 73, 78, 87, 89, 93, 95, 97

C

Caesar 25
Cajuns ix
Cambis 76
Canada ix, xiv, 3, 20, 24, 80, 85, 90
Canso xvi, xviii, 27, 30, 31, 32, 33, 35,
    37, 39, 44, 45, 47
Cape Breton ix, x, xvii, 5, 27, 38, 40, 44,
    46, 47, 49, 50, 54, 59, 69
Cape Breton Island xvii, 5, 27, 54, 69
Cape Elizabeth 19
Cape Porpoise 19
Cape Sable Indians 3. See also Mi'kmaq
Casco Bay 15, 23, 28, 38, 48
Catholicism xiv, 5, 24
Catholic religious orders xv, 5
Chebucto harbor 49, 53, 54
Chedabucto 27
Chignecto xvii, 9, 14, 18, 19, 29, 40, 41,
    42, 44, 49, 50, 52, 53, 56, 59, 63,
    65, 66, 67, 72, 75, 79, 80, 85
Chignecto Bay 9
chivalry, age of xiii
Chubb, Pasco 15, 16
Church, Benjamin 2, 9, 10, 11, 13, 16,
    18, 19, 20, 21, 89

Cobequid 42, 48
Cocagne 71
Columbus, Christopher xiv
Compagnies Franches de la Marine 42
Cook, James 76
Cope, Jean-Baptiste 52, 58, 59, 91
Corne, Louis de la 41
Cornwallis, Edward 51, 52, 53, 58,
    73, 90
coureur des bois 13
Crecy xiii
Crown of England xiv

D

Danks's Rangers 68, 71
Dark Ages xii
Dartmouth 54, 55, 56, 57, 76
Deerfield 20, 21, 22, 24
d'Estourmel, Constantin-Louis 49
de Vergor, Louis Du Pont Duchambon
    60, 64, 79
d'Iberville, Pierre Le Moyne 15
dikes 22
Dudley, Joseph, 21
Dummer, William 35
Dunston, Hannah 25
Duquesnel, Jean-Baptiste-Louis Le
    Prévost 44
Duvivier, Francois Dupont 45

E

Eastern Canada ix
Eastern Indians 9, 19, 28
Eneas (Maliseet), 28
England xi, xii, xiii, xiv, xv, xvi, 1, 2, 3,
    5, 6, 7, 8, 9, 11, 12, 13, 14, 17, 19,
    20, 21, 22, 23, 25, 26, 27, 28, 31,
    32, 34, 35, 36, 37, 39, 40, 45, 46, 47,
    49, 51, 52, 55, 63, 64, 66, 68, 69, 70,
    73, 76, 81, 84, 85, 88
English ix, xi, xiii, xiv, xv, xvi, 1, 2, 3, 4,
    5, 6, 7, 8, 9, 10, 11, 12, 13, 14, 15,
    16, 17, 18, 19, 20, 22, 23, 24, 25, 26,

Forty-fifth Regiment 55
France xi, xii, xiii, xiv, xv, 3, 5, 6, 11, 12,
    13, 14, 19, 20, 21, 23, 24, 25, 26, 27,
    29, 30, 31, 37, 40, 42, 44, 47, 48, 49,
    50, 52, 55, 58, 59, 60, 65, 66, 69,
    70, 73, 74, 76, 77, 78, 80, 83, 88,
    89, 90, 91, 93, 95
Frankfort 70
Franklin, Michael 59
French ix, xiii, xiv, xv, xvi, xvii, xviii, 2,
    3, 4, 5, 6, 7, 8, 9, 10, 11, 12, 13, 14,
    15, 16, 17, 18, 19, 20, 21, 22, 23, 24,
    25, 26, 27, 28, 29, 30, 31, 32, 33, 34,
    36, 37, 40, 41, 42, 43, 44, 45, 46,
    47, 48, 49, 50, 51, 52, 53, 54, 55, 56,
    57, 59, 60, 61, 62, 63, 64, 65, 66, 67,
    68, 69, 70, 71, 72, 74, 76, 77, 78, 79,
    80, 82, 83, 87, 88, 89, 90, 93, 97
French Crown 6, 19
French Lake 72
Fresnière, Joseph-Francois Hertel de
    la 10
Frye, Joseph 61
furs xiii, xv, 4
fur trade 2, 5, 13, 83

G

Gaspé x, 73
Gaspereau Valley 42
Gates, Horatio 52
Gaulin, Antoine 26
George's Island 75
Georgetown 34
Gettysburg 87
Glode, Ballomy 80
Goat Island 48
Gorham, John 45
Gorham's Rangers 45, 48, 56, 68
Governing Council 37, 52
Grand-Pré xviii, 14, 21, 22, 41, 42, 43,
    44, 49, 50, 56, 57, 79, 91
gray 42
Great Britain xii, xvi, 19, 44, 49, 50, 55,
    60, 69, 81, 88, 91

Great Swamp Fight 10
Grimross 67, 72
Guysborough 13, 27
Gyles, John 17, 22, 23, 34, 37, 48

H

Halifax xvi, xvii, xviii, 51, 52, 54, 56,
    57, 58, 59, 65, 70, 72, 75, 76, 80,
    87, 90, 95
Hamilton, John 57
Hanfield, John 65
Haverhill 12, 25
Hillsborough River 41
Hopson, Peregrine 58
Howe, Edward 52
Howe, William 76
Hudson Bay 27
Huguenot 30, 90
Hundred Years' War xiii
Huron 13, 47, 69

I

Illinois 31, 69
indigenous peoples 5
Intermarriage 5
Iroquoian xi
Iroquois 2, 5, 12, 24, 25
Isle Royale 27, 50, 71
Isle Saint-Jean 27, 40, 41, 47, 49, 50, 71

J

Jacobites 53
James II (king) 13
Jeddore 33, 34, 59
Jemseg 12, 72
Jesuits 5, 31
John Payzant 75
Johnson, William 63
Jonquière, Marquis de 49
Joseph (Maliseet) 28

K

Kahnawake 24

wood xii
Wyandot 20

X

Xavier, Francois 37

Y

York 10, 14, 21, 27
Yorktown 87